When da vinci came

Sajjad YazdanPanah

Title: When da vinci came

Author: Sajad YazdanPanah (Sajjad YazdanPanah)

ISBN: 9781939123367

Library Congress Control Number (LCCN): 2014922363

Publisher: Supreme Century, Los Angeles, CA, USA

Prepare for Publishing: Asan Nashr

www.ASANASHR.com

From Author with Love:

I am Sajjad Yazdanpanah . I was born Iran, in Shiraz city, 23.02.1986.

I am Writer, Journalist and scriptwriter. I offer and present this book first to all young and teenagers around the world and for oppressed people of Iran and I wish one day be exited Iran and all other countries which are in Human Right Watch's black list, and to regard democracy like USA and I wish one-day Islamic government regime fail in Iran and the political and religious prisoners be released and executions stop in all around the world.

I wrote this book a mixture of fiction, social and political issues. I endeavored to write this book entertained and interesting for readers.

And finally I am thankful of supreme century publisher for publishing my book.

 contact me: sajad1986@gmail.com

facebook: sajad_sky@yahoo.com

Roy and David were in the metro. They were on the way to come back home. Roy was studying economics and David psychology. They were still continuing their close relationships for their old friendship at high school and also being at the same university. And even their different fields of study couldn't ruin their close relationship. They were talking with a slow tone , but excitingly about the courses and classes which they had on that day as if by these conversations they intended to reduce their tiredness of those classes. "How were your classes today?" asked Roy. "They were too boring. Having three major and difficult courses in one day can make someone very tired. How were your classes?" said David. "Not bad. One of my professors assigned me a research and I must prepare it up to two weeks. By the way when he told me its subject , I slightly became surprised. I wanted to tell him that I was not ready to do such a research , but I was afraid he thought I couldn't do this task and I was a lazy student," said Roy. "Oh , don't worry boy , you can do it," said David. "But I don't think I can present a good and acceptable research about globalizing the economy," said Roy. "You know, Roy. You are always afraid of doing hard work, but when you get down to it, you see it's not so difficult that you think," said David. "Forget about it. It's better to talk about other things. But before we go to another issue, I want to tell you a point or maybe a joke. Once I read in a psychological article that a psychologist re commended his patients to suppose their problems in the form of a creature. In order to solve their problems and they laugh at this creature so much that those problems become trivial before their eyes. When I thought about the relation of this point with ourselves, I came to this conclusion that whenever we fail a course, we should laugh at this being or in fact at our problems like those people who laugh at every thing even at the crack of the wall ," said Roy. "Okay, but it's better to keep the recommendation of that psychologist for the end of the term," said David with a smile. Then David brought his head near Roy's ear as if he wanted to whisper something in his ear and said, "Roy, look at that tall boy who sat there right now. See how long his hands and legs are. They reminds me of my of my childhood's modeling paste playing." Roy, who was waiting for something to laugh at, couldn't control himself from excessive laugh. Then as if he intended to offer David satirical power by saying something funnier than David's words, he whispered to David, "David! Look at that woman who sits down there and is reading newspaper. The newspaper which she holds in her hands is two times bigger than her body. As if instead of she reads the newspaper, the newspaper is reading her." They laugh in a manner that one thinks the world is given to them. The interesting point was that no one knew at what they were laughing except themselves. The distance between the university and home was too long for both of them and it took about 45 minutes to travel through the distance between the university and home or vice versa. And almost much of this time was spending in the metro. So both of them tried to use their time in a good way and spend it by laughing, talking and most often by playing computer games. Then Roy brought out his laptop computer from his bag and said to David, "David, I want to surprise you today. Because today's games are different from past days." "So what?" asked David. "Finally, I subscribe to a game net server. At any time of the day and night I can play the games online and more than one player by paying 45 dollars every month," implied Roy. Roy, who was using wireless internet service, after connecting to the internet connected to his intended server and after entering his account username and password played a game in the online game server. "You know David, surprising you is mainly related to the time when we go out of the server," said Roy. "Are you serious?" asked David . "Yes," implied Roy. One of the most prominent interests of them was computer games and this common ground intensified their friendship. During playing the game time passed so quickly that playing for 35 minutes seemed to them as 10 minutes. When the train arrived at their destination they couldn't believe that they were really at the destination. Roy went out of the game server and put his laptop computer in his bag quickly and both of them detrained. Their homes were just one street far from each other .So they return home with each other every day and detrain at the same station. "You know David, what is the main part of your surprising? On this paper I wrote the username and password of my account in the game server. You can use it, too," said Roy. "Oh, No. This is yours," said David. "I'm not always playing the game. I just play 3 hours a day, so what about the other times of a day? Anyhow I pay for the 14 hours online games, so it's better to accept it. You can use it whenever that you like," said Roy. "Okay. I accept it, but I think no one can have a friend like you all over the world," said David. Then suddenly Roy said to David loudly, "David, look at that boy on the other side of the street who is skating. How he exerts himself to move." "Yes, he moves as if he pulls a 2 tons automobile," said David while laughing. "If he participates in the contest of the world strongest men, he will be the first certainly," said Roy with an excessive laugh. They were still laughing and talking when they arrived on the street which Roy lives and after saying good bye, they left. It seemed that nothing could ruin their intimacy and happiness. They used to come back home with each other. Even they moved in a manner that they didn't intend to leave each other. Their laughing affected them so much that removed their daily tiredness. They usually came to the university alone, but always came back with each other. They behaved like the school children not the students of the university. At last Roy arrived home. "Hello, Mom," said Roy. "Hi, Roy! How is today?" said Kathryn. "It was almost great," said Roy. "I think you become very tired as usual," said Kathryn. "No, not at all. What is tiredness? I never become tired of learning. Believe me that if the authorities of the university allow me, I will stay at the university even at nights," said Roy with a special smile as if he intended to kid with Kathryn. "You mean that you hate being at home so much?!" asked Kathryn . "No, Mom I said this because of my excessive interest of learning," implied Roy. "It's better for you not to chant a lot. Your lunch is on the kitchen table. I made a coup of coffee, too. But don't drink it before your lunch. The coffee is in the coffeepot. It just may become a little cold," said Kathryn. "Mom, it's better not to give me an ethical advice," said Roy. And then Roy drank two coups of coffee and changed his clothes and returned to the kitchen to eat his lunch. He turned on his mp3 player as usual and lay on his bed. He made the volume of his mp3 player so much loud that he couldn't hear the sounds around him .several minutes passed. He closed his eyes and wanted to sleep that suddenly saw his mother standing in front of him and was calling him, "Roy ... Roy..." And he, who knew that his mother was there, took out the head phones and said, "What mom? Why don't you let me to rest?" "I called you, but you didn't answer and I be came worried," implied Kathryn. "What made you worried? I'm not a child," said Roy. "I told you that because you didn't answer me, I thought something bad may happen to you," said Kathryn. "Don't be upset. I want to tell you something." "What do you want to say?" asked Roy . "Tonight one of your dad's friends, Mr. Johnson, will come to our house with his family," said Kathryn. "But Dad doesn't still come back from work. So how did you know that?" said Roy. "He came just some minutes ago, but you didn't hear his voice. I thought if you are aware of this matter, your studying won't be disrupted," said Kathryn with a special smile. "Don't worry, Mom! Your son is a full-fledged genius. My plans never are disrupted," Roy said in a manner that it was obvious that he was kidding. "I hope so. If you want, you can sleep again my dear! I just woke you up because I was worried," said Kathryn. "No problem. I wanted to wake up soon," said Roy. "By the way, why didn't you eat your lunch, Roy?" asked Kathryn . "I'm not hungry," implied Roy. "Eat your lunch, Roy," said Kathryn. "Okay. I will eat it some minutes later," said Roy. Then both of them went to the kitchen. "Hello, Dad!" said Roy . And Steven said while eating his lunch, "Hi, Roy! How are you?" "I'm fine," replied Roy. "Did Kathryn tell you that tonight Mr. Johnson and his family are going to our house?" asked Steven. "Yes, she said," said Roy. "He is a big shot man. He is one of the biggest stock holders of bourse. It is about months that he socializes with our insurance company. To tell you the truth he has a very good relationship with me. During several past months he became much more intimate with me. It's along time that we intend to establish a family relationship with each other by his suggestion. I like you to be present at this party," said Steven. "Sure Dad. If you want, I will go certainly," said Roy. "I said I like, I didn't want to force you," said Steven. "I also didn't say that you want to force me," said Roy. "In fact I behaved in this manner for he is an important person. I knew him from long time ago that our relationship intensified by chance." "I know Dad. But the most important people of the world for me are you and Mom. Dad! You as a chief of a big insurance company aren't unimportant. More over, the honesty and sincerity that you have can rarely be found in others. It's natural that the other people want to make their relationships with you more," said Roy. "Any way, he is really an important man, my son. The major share of some big companies owes to him," said Steven.

"Now, I understand what you mean. So tonight we have a very special and important party. Those people who go around with bodyguards and bullet proof cars!" said Roy. "I'm happy that you understand what I mean," said Steven. "By the way, at what time they will come?" asked Roy . "At seven o' clock," replied Steven. Then Roy returned to his room and after a short rest, engaged in studying his lessons on that day. It was 5 o' clock in the afternoon. He had studied for several hours, but due to his excessive love of studying, he didn't become tired of studying at all. Although he didn't still become tired of studying, he relinquished studying since he studied all of his daily materials several times. Then he decided to play his favorite computer games. Playing computer games is considered as the most interesting and attractive Roy's hobby. Because he was interested in computer games from child hood and didn't have much interest in group or motion games such as football , baseball , basketball , … for this reason it seemed that computer games and generally the computer are the inherent part of Roy's life

Even his mother and father knew this fact well . Roy played for about an hour and then searched on the web about the research that he must submit to his professor up to two weeks later and he could find most of his required materials in less than five minutes. Then he turned off his computer and cleaned his room. He wore one of his best clothes which were a black suit. It was 6:45 and he was preparing himself for the guests. Roy's family was not such a social family and it happened rarely that a guest come to their house. Most of their relatives were living in other cities and only his grandparents that were Steven's father and mother and one of Roy's uncles lived in New York. Due to this fact celebrating a party is very exciting and interesting for all of them specially Roy. By referring to the words that his father said about the guests, Roy was aware that these guests should be different from the others. A plain party with common people is also exciting for Roy and his family what if such an important person is going to come to their house. The guests were with in to come and Roy's anxiety was increasing. Each three persons became completely ready in order not to shy in front of their new guests. Roy thought so much that he will spend difficult hours. Because of the way that Steven described the guests, Roy supposed that he should sit like a bogy and think for a long time that a word or sentence came to his mind and start talking with them. Three of them were sitting in the living room and watching television. It was five minutes to seven; they had a special eagerness for coming of the guests. Finally the clock reached seven and while several seconds passed from seven o'clock, the bell rang. The father picked up the receiver and when he saw them on the monitor of the eye phone, said with a tone which seemed that he was happy, "They finally come." Roy's thought was right. An expensive automobile was parked in front of the house's yard and two body guards were also with them. Then they parked the car in the yard of the house. But his guess about their appearance was completely wrong. Mr. Johnson came with a completely different appearance than Roy thought. He wore jeans and sport shoes. One of the body guards was sitting in the car and the other in the yard. They became relax since no danger threatened Mr. Johnson and his family there. After greeting, they sat in the saloon. A silence was dominated for several seconds. But Mr. Johnson started speaking unadvisedly. The others also began to talk. After some minutes Mr. Johnson's daughter whispered something to Mr. Johnson. Then her father said with a special excitement, "Kathy is saying that she is studying at the same university and field with Roy. You know what is strange for me? That they are studying at the same university and field, but don't know each other. Of course Kathy knows Roy." Then Roy said, "To tell you the truth, our university is very big. You should forgive me not to know your daughter. Thousands of students educate at our university that even a large number of them come from other countries. For this reason most of us don't know each other. But I think I saw your daughter before." After that Kathy and Roy, who were trying to confer with each other about the proposed matter, started talking unadvisedly. "Mr. Douglas, I saw you in the macro economics class today. You accepted to do a research about globalizing the economy," said Kathy while looking at Roy. "Yes, that's right. So you and I are studying at the same field," said Roy. Then these conversations continued by them about university and courses until they finally changed their subject of talk .Roy couldn't say some thing to Kathy which was not related to the university and courses. But when Kathy said that it's better to talk about other things, he became relax. "Like what subjects?" asked Roy. "Subjects such as music, your hobbies and favorite programs," replied Kathy. "What is your favorite style of music?" asked Kathy. "First, rock and then pop and metal," said Roy. "But, in general I like every style of music which is good and effective." "I myself also like most of music styles, but I like techno and pop more than the others," said Kathy. Roy's initial anxiety for confronting with guests reduced. The guests were too different from what Roy thought and this made Roy become happy and thrilling. Roy's parents were also talking to Kathy's parents as if they knew each other for several years. After Roy's mother hosted the guests, they became surprised that why Roy's family did not have a servant. And when Kathy's parents asked Steven and Kathryn the reason of this matter, they clearly said that they did not like to employ a servant at all and they didn't need a servant. Roy's family was rich, but they never agreed with employing a servant. It was 8:30 and they started eating dinner. After eating dinner, Kathy asked Roy something that was to some extent childish in Roy's opinion, and he didn't expect it. "Roy, don't you mind if I want to see your room?" asked Kathy. Roy, who be came surprised with this request, said after several seconds of delay, "okay, I will be glad to do so." And then they went to Roy's room. "How a big book case you have!" said Kathy . "To tell you the truth I don't like to borrow my required books from the library. So I always try to buy my required or favorite books. But the thing which caused Kathy to be surprised more than any thing else was that Roy used a big plasma monitor instead of a usual monitor. And on his computer desk instead of a small monitor, a big plasma monitor was showing off." "Don't you think that your computer is to some extent unusual?" said Kathy . "Oh, now I get it. It is surprising to every one that instead of a small LCD monitor I use a big plasma monitor. But this way the images are seemed much more real. Especially at the time of playing, the achieved excitement is several times more than the same playing with small monitors," said Roy. "So you also do play!" said Kathy . "Yes, I like computer games so much," said Roy. Another thing that attracted Kathy's attention was a rather big aquarium in which beautiful types of fish were seen. "You also have an aquarium in your room! What a happy morale and good taste you have!" said Kathy. "The existence of an aquarium in the room makes someone feel relax, moreover I like fish and generally aquarium fish," said Roy. Then they sat on the sofa which was in the middle of Roy's room. "Why your room is too big?" asked Kathy. "At first I didn't want to have such a big room, but it became big accidentally," said Roy. "You mean that you changed your room to a big one?" asked Kathy. "Oh, no. I didn't mean this. At first I chose one of the small rooms of our house as my room, but after a couple of days I liked this room. Because it is big and light in almost all hours of the day. The window of this room is toward the south, so it's light in all hours of the day. And as I like natural light so much, I chose this room as my room," said Roy. Some kinds of magazine and newspaper were observed on the table which was in front of them. "Do you like magazines and newspapers so much?" asked Kathy. "Yes, what about you?" said Roy. "I read magazines and newspapers, but not the same as you do. I don't read the newspapers daily and about the magazine I should say that I just read one kind of it. But you buy a lot of newspapers and magazines every day and week, don't you?" said Kathy . "That's right. I like the press very much," said Roy. It could be easily understood that Roy like the press so much by a lot of magazines and newspapers which were on his table. Then Kathy asked Roy about the research which he was supposed to submit to his professor as if she intended to help him. "By the way what are you going to do about the research that you accepted?" asked Kathy. "It's nearly finished. Just some diagrams are remained that I will draw them at the end of the work," said Roy. "Really?" asked Kathy. "You cannot believe it?" said Roy. "Yes, but … did you really do your research so rapidly?" said Kathy. "Well. Yes. I got part of it from internet and found another part of it in a book which is in my book shelf. It just needs to be arranged and generalized." "How much time do you study in a day?" asked Kathy. "If you mean studying my textbooks 3 to 4 hours a day, but about the other books I should say as much as I can and have energy and patience." After some minutes they returned to the living room. Then Roy brought his laptop computer and began playing. When Roy entered the game server and started his favorite game, he saw that most of the stages were completed successfully and he became so happy that suddenly said to himself quietly, "It's magnificent, David . Excellent! You are really terrific." "Did you say something, Roy? Are you with me?" asked Kathy . "Oh, no. I apologize, I'm not with you," said

Roy. Roy told Kathy while playing the game, "Do you want to play, Kathy?" "I'm not sure. Because I really don't like computer games so much," replied Kathy. "Try it once. Maybe you like it," said Roy. "Well, okay," said Kathy. Although Kathy did not know a lot about that game, she started playing. "It's very good. It's really great for the first time," said Roy. After Kathy played for several minutes, Roy continued the game again. "It was very exciting," said Kathy. "You have a very well talent," said Roy. Then Roy turned off his laptop and they talked with each other again. "Do you have class tomorrow?" asked Kathy. "Yes," replied Roy. "Can I see your class schedule?" asked Kathy. "Of course," said Roy. Roy went to his room and brought the paper on which the list of his classes was written and gave it to Kathy. "How is your classes' schedule?" asked Roy. "It is almost the same as yours. But I don't have class on Friday," replied Kathy. Mr. Johnson and his family left their house at 9:30 and the party came to end at last. The day after that day when Roy wanted to come back home from the university, he saw a silver G.T ford which was parked near him on the front street of the university. That was Kathy. Kathy asked Roy to get in the car. Roy made his attempt not to accept her request, because he was waiting for David and wanted to come back home with him. But Kathy repeated her request several times and at last Roy got in the car. Roy wondered that why Kathy herself did not drive the car and he asked her the reason of this matter. And Kathy said that she had a driving license, but since she didn't like driving, she drove rarely and because of this most often her body guard drove the car instead of her. On that day although Roy didn't have any bad feelings toward Kathy, he also didn't have such a good feeling. Along the way to come back home he thought all the time that may be he offended David. But when he thought about his special friendship with David and also the high intimacy between himself and David, he became relieved. He knew that the friendship between him and David couldn't be weakened by a little misunderstanding. When he arrived home, he was not in a good mood as if he missed someone or forgot doing something. 15 minutes later Roy got home and David called him. "Hello," said David. "Hi," said Roy. "I was worried about you," said David. "NO, to tell you the truth today one of my friends asked me to take me home accidentally. I tried a lot not to accept it, but I couldn't. Any way, I hope you don't become upset," said Roy. "Oh, no boy. I just became worried about you," said David. "By the way you did an excellent play. You passed one of the most difficult stages for me. Last night when I entered my account in the game server and start playing that game, I became very excited. I didn't think that you are such a professional player," said Roy. "No, I'm not professional; I'm just a simple player," said David. "Any way, you did it very well. Well, thanks for calling me. Don't you want to say anything else?" said Roy. The friendship of Roy and David was so old and strong that Roy's parents, especially his mother knew David well and sometimes asked Roy about David's condition in order to be aware of his condition. After David called, Roy's mother became a little curious as if she heard Roy's words with

David on the phone. "Was that David?" asked Kathryn . "Yes," replied Roy. "Is something wrong?" asked Kathryn . "No, Mom. To tell you the truth, you know that every day I come back home with David, but today I couldn't come with David and he became worried about me since he didn't see me," replied Roy. "Dear, I don't want to interfere in your affairs, but can I ask that with whom you came back today?" asked Kathryn. "Yes, with Kathy Johnson. But she didn't drive the car herself. Her body guard drove," said Roy. "She is a kind girl. From now you have anther friend like David. By the way I want to tell you good news," said Kathryn. "What news?!" asked Roy. "Your grandfather will come to our house tonight," said Kathryn. "Really? Did he come back from trip?!" asked Roy. "Yes, he himself said that he came back one week ago, but he wanted to surprise us. So he didn't tell us that he had returned," replied Kathryn. "Have you told this to Dad?" asked Roy. "Yes, I called him one hour ago. When he heard this news, he became so happy," said Kathryn. Then Roy went to his room. He lay on his bed to rest. He felt sleepy, but did not want to sleep. After several minutes he sat at his desk in order to study the things that he learned at the university. Those times that he felt tiredness, he didn't usually study at the desk and he studied on the bed or sofa. Because sitting at the desk for long hours was very boring for him. He sat at the desk for about half an hour , but then he picked up the book which he was studying and put it on the bed and lay on the bed and continued his study . He felt tiredness, but he wanted to continue his study. So he continued studying up to 45 minutes later. He learned all of the materials of that day well, so he closed his book and collected his notes and pamphlets and put them on his desk. This time he lay on the bed to sleep. He was very relieved because he learned all of his materials well and reviewed them several times. He slept, but his sleeping did not last for along time and after 25 minutes he woke up. He went to the kitchen to drink a coup of coffee. He understood that his father came back from work. He said hello to his father and after drinking a coup of coffee, went back to his room and turned on his computer and started playing the game. He continued playing up to 2 hours. After a short rest, he reviewed the materials which he had studied some hours ago. Then while his favorite music was played loudly from the computer, he started studying his favorite magazines and continued reading them for almost an hour. Then he turned off the computer. He felt moodiness. He usually goes on an excursion with David two or three times a week. On the occasions that he felt boring a lot, he went on an excursion with David .But totally he didn't like excursion and going out so much .Any way he decided to call David and go to him .After he called him and became sure that he was at home and didn't go any where, went to him by bicycle. First they talked for some minutes in front of David's house. While they were talking, a girl came out of the house and said something to David and then went. "Who was that girl?" asked Roy. "She is my sister, Sara .Don't' you know her?!" said David. "You had told me that you have a sister who is 2 years older than you, but I haven' seen her since now," said Roy. "She is the accountant of a company," said David. "Forget about it .I just asked because I didn't know her," said Roy. Then they continued talking while walking on the street. "By the way, my grandfather wants to come to our house tonight," said Roy. "A man whom you said is a tourist and traveled to Africa?" asked David. "Yes, it is a week that he returned. Although he is 68 years old, he is very energetic. He can have a quite and safe life like those who have the same age. But always he seeks excitement and danger. He also loves traveling." "Say what kinds of traveling, traveling to Africa," said David. "You know why he has chosen Africa? Because he loves wild life. He likes jungle parks and wild animals so much. Although watching the wild animals from a near distance is very dangerous, he enjoys it and has done this task several times," said Roy. They were walking until they arrived at a park near their house. They sat on a bench for several minutes and continued their talks. Then both of them returned home. But on the way to come back home Roy thought about David's sister unconsciously. Although he didn't have any special feeling to her, her image repeated in his mind successively. Roy had a strange feeling. He didn't have such feeling yet by seeing a girl .But it seemed that from the moment that Roy had seen Sara this strange feeling was imbued in him that he thought about her unconsciously. After a few minutes was passed from the time that Roy came home, his mother came to his room to talk to him. "Did you go to David?" asked Kathryn. "Yeah, we walked with each other and talked," replied Roy.   "David is a very good boy. I'm so glad that you have such a friend," said Kathryn. "Yeah Mom, I don't know with whom I should walk when I feel moodiness if I did not have such a friend like David," said Roy. Then Kathryn said while she wanted to go out of Roy's room, "It's about time that grandpa turns up." Then Kathryn went to the living room and engaged in watching TV. And in the meantime, she started talking to Steven. This was the usual habit of Roy's parents to talk about the daily works and Roy and Steven's work affairs or everything which was related to their family and life and Roy was a ware of this relative good behavior of his parents. When Roy was hearing their talks and understood that how his parents had mutual agreement, he became satisfied to have such a family heartily and was proud of them. It was 6:45 in the afternoon. Since it was October, the days were short and it was completely dark outside. Although Roy saw Sara about one hour ago, he felt that it was a few seconds ago. As it a strong sense wanted to weigh on his mind to Sara. Wherever he looked at or every task that he wanted to do, Sara's face appeared in his mind. When he was thinking about Sara, his heart beat fast and without wanting to cry, tear drops were falling from his eyes involuntarily. It was very hard for him to believe, but he was fallen in love. Every thing was happened in a moment. As if Roy was involved in an event involuntarily that he himself did not have any role in its occurring. Now he knows well that he loves Sara. But he was an introverted and careful boy and although he knew that he was in love with Sara, he tried to hide his love. The thing which was strange for him was that why these sentimental transitions were occurred only by seeing Sara. Any way, whether it was strange or not, Roy was fallen in love with Sara. But because of various reasons he decided to hide his love feelings. Sara was the sister of one of his most intimate and best friends and he knew that maybe by expressing his love to Sara their friendship finished forever. This hypothesis would become more intense if Sara did not love Roy. But there were other reasons as well. Maybe Roy's parents or Sara's parents would not agree with this marriage. Because Sara was 2 years older than Roy. Roy was engaged in considering all aspects of his thoughts and feelings, when the bell rang. As usual Roy answered the eye phone. He rapidly went to the eye phone which was almost 20 meters far from his room and picked up the receiver of the eye phone. In the monitor of the eye phone he saw his grandfather and grandmother. "Who's that, Roy?" asked Kathryn. "They are grandpa and grandma," said Roy. And Kathryn said happily, "Finally they come," After greetings and welcome all of them gathered in the living room. An excessive happiness can be seen obviously on their faces. Grandfather had a lot of things to say. In most of their words he talked about missing Steven and his family. He carried a number of albums of his travel photographs that he explained each of them a lot. The way of grandpa's look at them revealed that he couldn't describe those excitements and beauties which he had seen in the pure nature of Africa. Every body was listening to his talks about the photographs and his trip. Before they had dinner, grandpa spoke a lot about his trip. It was 8 o'clock. All of them were hungry. Kathryn went to the kitchen now and then and all of them knew that she would surprise them with her various and delicious foods as usual. At the dinner table grandpa and grandma were too happy that their little family gathered again after so long time and they express this happiness to Roy and his parents .After eating dinner Roy was still thinking about grandpa's words of his trip and his words were so interesting and exciting that he forget one of the most important thing of grandpa's trip .Roy did not think about the gift at all. Their meeting was so joyful that Roy forget the gift completely .when grandpa uttered the "gift", he became surprised. Grandpa brought out a necklace from his bag and gave it to Roy. "I know Roy that you are thinking now that what is this gift that I brought for you .If I were you, I certainly think just about the gift, " said grandpa. Then he gave the beautiful necklace to Roy that it can be easily understood that its chain is gold and it was made from precious stone. "You are my only grandson. I hope it is worthy of you," said grandpa. Roy, who became so happy, said, "oh, my grandpa, it's very beautiful .I don't know that I can really accept it or not, It seems that it's very expensive." "You are getting me sad, boy. Who is able not to accept a gift? If you don't accept it, I will be so upset. You don't know how long I talked to its owner that he agreed to sell it .I'm not superstitious, but its owner be lived that this necklace has a magical effect. For this reason I hardly could buy it .At least I like you to accept it," said grandpa. "Accept, Roy .do not try to reject grandpa's gift," said Steven. And Roy took the necklace from grandpa and said, "Thanks a lot, grandpa." And then grandpa said, "I hope you'll

like it .I couldn't find any thing better than this."
Then he brought out a very delicate and relatively
small piece of cloth from a small sachet that he
carried with himself on which a painting was drawn
and he gave it to Steven and Kathryn .The size of the
cloth was as similar as the size of a relatively small
painting picture. Grandpa also prepared a number of
films that by spending some money he changed the
films which he had recorded by his handy cam to
DVD. There was not enough time to watch all of the
films. Although grandpa showed them just the
important and main parts of the films, it lasted two
hours that grandpa showed them those films, It was
11'o clock, but time passed so quickly that they
couldn't believe it was 11 o'clock. Grandpa and
Grandma said goodbye to them and came back home
that was less than half an hour far from their house.
They went, but the tone of grandpa's speaks still
remained in the minds of them as if grandpa is still
there and is explaining about his trip for them. That
night they learned an important point that how a long
time journey can affect the human's life and morale

and how it can give energy and excitement to the human. Roy was lying on his bed to start his night sleep. He was still thinking about Sara and this caused him to sleep a little later than the other nights. It was hard for him to accept that he was fallen in love with Sara. Before this event , marriage or mutual love were unimportant for Roy and these matters were so unimportant for Roy and these matters were so unimportant for him that he did not think about marriage at all and in his opinion there were issues much more important than marriage that he never thought about this. Before this, he just engaged himself in educational development and doing entertaining and interesting programmes. Especially computer games and entertainments formed a major part of his amusements. But now it seems that a revolution was made in side him. He tried so much to forget his feelings toward Sara, but it seemed that his effort was useless. Because thinking about Sara prevented him from thinking about anything else. When Roy remembered Sara's face or the moment that he had seen her, his heart beat so fast that he felt his heart would come out of his chest. Or tears dropped from his eyes without being upset of something or crying. Accepting these situations was so difficult for Roy because he was rational and realistic and he was not a person who decided according to his feelings. And this matter that he was suddenly defeated by his feelings toward Sara annoyed him slightly. It was not completely light when Roy woke up. He was off on that day because he didn't have any classes at the university, but he always used to wake up early in the morning. He took a glance at his watch which he had put near his pillow in order not to be forced to look at the table clock or the clock on the wall when he got up. It was 6:45 that is, there was still half an hour to the time that he set the clock on and it was interesting that everyday woke up almost 30 minutes later than this time and after the clock rang for several minutes. But today he got up without the ringing of the clock and 30 minutes earlier than usual, while he slept late last night. He himself had surprised that he woke up so early in the morning. Unlike everyday he didn't feel drowsy. He got out of his bed and went to the bath to wash his hands and face. Then he poured some coffee and water in the coffeepot in order to make coffee and after that came back to his room and lay on his bed, but he didn't feel sleepy. The sky was becoming light soon. Several minutes passed and it was completely light. Roy's room window was toward the east. For this reason as soon as the sunrise the room became too light. Passing the light rays of sun from the aquarium which was in front of the window made beautiful lights like a rainbow in the wall, in front of the window. Roy had become glad by seeing these beautiful and colorful lights. It was obvious that this scene has existed everyday in Roy's room, but Roy paid attention to it just on that day. Roy had still a bee in his bonnet about Sara. As if he looked at every where, he saw Sara's picture. He was thinking with himself that Kathryn entered the room. When she saw that Roy was awake, became surprised a little and said, "Are you awake, my dear?" "Hi, Mom. Yeah, today I wake up a bit earlier than every day," said Roy. "Did you make coffee?" asked Kathryn. "Yes," answered Roy. "You forgot to turn it off. You are lucky that I arrived on time," said Mom. They went to the kitchen. Steven woke up, too and he was also in the kitchen. "You are a strange boy, Roy! One day you sleep so deep that the sound of a bomb cannot wake you up and one day you wake up earlier than your mother wants to wake up you, "said Kathryn. They went out of the kitchen after eating breakfast and drinking coffee. Steven went to his work and Kathryn and Roy went to their rooms. Roy lay on his bed for a while and then started studying his lessons. Although learning the materials was not difficult for him, he did not have the usual concentration and felt that they became slightly difficult for him. The matters, which caused Roy to laugh in the past, now became the most important matters of Roy's life. He thought that these things were existed only in the books, myths or romantic films, but now he himself was involved in these matters. He tried a lot to concentrate all of his senses and energy on his daily tasks, but it seemed that he couldn't suppress his feelings. He was engaged in studying. Although he didn't have enough concentration, he continued studying. And he continued studying for almost 2 hours. Then he watched TV for a while and started studying again. He reviewed the materials which he had studied in the morning. Every thing was okay, but it seemed that time passed so slowly. Then he decided to play his favorite computer game online. But that day was seemed to be different from the other days. Even he didn't have enough concentration in playing the game and game stages had become more difficult for him than every day. It became more strange to Roy that he felt time was passing so slowly. Everyday when he played his favorite games, time was passing so quickly for him that when he came to himself, he understood that several hours passed. But that day was different. Roy was still playing and in his opinion a long time should pass, but when he looked at the clock, he saw that only twenty minutes had passed. Computer game couldn't amuse him and he gave up the idea of playing a game. This time he decided to listen to his favorite music, but every music that he listened to made him boring and did not satisfy him as usual. Until that moment time had passed so slowly for him that he felt a whole day had passed. But when he looked at the clock, it was 9:30 in the morning. After some minutes he decided to listen to online music, but soon he changed his mind. Even internet television, that most often he watched his favorite channels in this way, couldn't amuse him. And he finally turned off the computer, it was strange for himself that his common entertainments couldn't amuse him and they became boring for him. He was not also in a mood to read newspaper and magazine. He walked in the home for a while. He walked without any purpose in the home. The way he was looking and walking was like that he was seeing a special person in every part of the house or was looking at a particular person. He seemed to be moodiness. Finally he returned to his room. As if a day was changed to a month for him. He took a glance at the clock; it was 9:40 in the morning. From the moment that he had started his daily activity a number of questions were asked in his mind automatically and continually: Does Sara think about me now? Does she feel like me after meeting me? And questions like these. Roy did a lot of works on that day. He studied his lessons completely and even he reviewed them and; in short, he had done all of the works that he should do in one day. But the hands of the clock did not still reach 10. He himself knew that he loves Sara, but tried to suppress this feeling. Sometimes he tried to justify his unusual condition by answering to the questions which were asked in his mind constantly. But he did not want to deceive himself anymore. Therefore he decided to go to David and get some information about Sara's work place indirectly. If he could communicate with her secretly or at least be sure that his love to Sara was not unilateral and she also loves him, he would be more relaxed. So he decided to go to David. He was aware that David's classes schedule was matched totally with his classes and he didn't have any classes on that day. But by just then he set in motion, this point came to his mind that maybe David became upset that he wanted to ask questions about his sister let alone such private questions in order to know his

44

sister's work place. So he changed his mind. Suddenly he remembered the gift which his grandfather gave to him and quickly brought it out of his trousers' pocket which he had worn last night. It was a beautiful necklace. It had an oval stone which was carved and polished skillfully and it was like a green eye with this difference that the two small circles were green instead of white .He liked to show it to David tomorrow. He put it around his neck and stood in front of the mirror. Its appearance was to some extent girlish, but beautiful. Roy said to himself, "If it was girlish, grandpa would not buy it for me." Then he took off the necklace. There were two nails on one of the walls of the room. Roy had hung a picture on those nails before, but since he had removed that picture, there wasn't anything on those nails at that time. And he hung the necklace more on the wall and as a decorative thing. Although Roy didn't have any problem in his life, loving Sara caused him to be a little anxious. Any how that difficult day passed. Tomorrow when Roy went to the university again, he felt a special happiness.

When he visited his friends and classmates again, he looked at them in away as if he had not seen them for months. In the break Kathy come to him first. No one was around them and they started talking with each other. "Hello, Mr. Smith. Are you fine?" said Kathy." "Hi. You can call me Roy .It's better," said Roy. "You can also call me Kathy. I want to tell you something. A few days ago I heard from the TV news that a number of Leonardo daVinci works will be exhibited in the museum of the city. Yesterday I went to the ticket selling place of the exhibition and bought a ticket for you .Today is the second day of the exhibition. Visiting hours are from 4 to 9 p.m., "said Kathy."Thanks Kathy," said Roy. "You mean that you want to come with me?" asked Kathy. "Not together. But we'll see each other in the exhibition," replied Roy. "On what time you'll get there?" asked Kathy. "Is five o' clock okay?" said Roy. "Yes, it's good .I'll see you at Five o' clock," said Kathy. "What about the cost of the ticket?" asked Roy. "Don't mind it," replied Kathy. "Thanks Kathy, but I should pay it to you," said Roy. "Oh, no. Forget about it," said Kathy "But... Kathy, "said Roy."Don't say anything else. It's an invitation," said Kathy. "Okay. Thanks," said Roy. Kathy gave one of the two tickets to Roy and said, "By the way the address of the exhibition is written on the back of the ticket, but I think you know there."Roy took a glance at the address and said quickly, "Yeah, I know it. Since now I have gone there several times. "This was the first time that Roy sat near Kathy. But it made on difference for Roy. How ever, he felt a special comfort Roy's feeling toward Kathy was the same as his feeling toward David and he was so happy that he had found another intimate and kind friend like David. But Kathy's feeling toward Roy was a little vague. In spite of a special intimacy that she had toward Roy, her behavior was a bit queer. And Roy felt this well. The break time finished and they went to their classes. During the class time Kathy was keeping an eye on Roy. She took a look at Roy's book and notes now and then and did whatever that Roy did. Although Roy's concentration was still disrupted by thinking about Sara, his talent and specially his intelligence caused him to learn the lessons well in the class and he still felt that they were too simple for him. When the class finished, Roy should come back home because he didn't have any other classes. Kathy didn't have any other classes, either. Kathy asked Roy to come back home with her .But Roy refused her request very politely. Because he liked to talk to David and returning home with him was a very good opportunity for him to speak to David or get more information about Sara. It seemed that Kathy became relatively upset when Roy refused her request and asked with a slow tone, "Is there any special reason that you don't want to come with me? Our home is located on the same route, so why don't you come with me? " "No, to tell you truth I always come back home with one of friends , David , and if I don't come back with him ,he will be offended .we chose our classes from the beginning of the term in a way that we can come back home with each other or even on some days go to the university together . I'm sorry, Kathy .I should go right now. Because David is certainly waiting for me in front of the university," said Roy. Then Roy said good bye to Kathy and went. Roy and David went to the metro station and after a while the train arrived .They got on the train. Roy had a queer feeling. It was a good opportunity for Roy to get some information about Sara unnoticeably. From the beginning, David knew that Roy had a little anxiety. Roy tried to be calm, but David was as always. David started his jokes soon after they got on the train. Roy tried to be serious. "What's wrong with you, Roy? Why are you like this   today? You always seek something to laugh at," said David. "Who tells that I'm not laughing? I laughed at all of your jokes," said Roy "Yeah, but I don't know why you are not as everyday?" said David .Roy made all of his effort that at last he could change the subject of his talks to occupational issues. Then under the pretext of knowing Sara's field of study, he got the name and address of the company which Sara worked in. "What do you intend to do after your graduation?" asked Roy. "I haven't thought about it yet, but I will likely work at a psychological clinic. What about you,

Roy?" said David. "Well, there are many choices for me, consisting from an economical consultant for investment in stock exchange to an accountant of a company. By the way what field did your sister educate in?" said Roy. "She was studying in field of accountancy," said David. "In which company does she work, now?" asked Roy. "NPC Company, on 23rd street, block 12," replied David .Then Roy changed the subject of discussion to the jokes and laughing again skillfully. And at the end they played online games as usual. This fact that they could play their favorite games in metro by using wireless internet technology and laptop computer with each other doubled their enjoyment of playing. Then they said goodbye to each other and went home. Roy was so happy that he could get the address of Sara's work place. Roy had decided to give up suppressing his feeling. He was aware that he should confront with fact sooner or later. When he arrived at home he was so happy. It was obvious from his face that Roy was so happy. A Happiness that he himself knew its reason. He was aware that since he had the name and address of the company, he could get the telephone number of that company by calling telephone directory. Although it seemed that Roy treated a little dauntlessly against his feelings toward Sara, he was so careful and wanted to hide this matter for at least a short time. He was so careful that even his parents would not become a ware of this matter. It was 11 o'clock in the morning. Roy dared himself to go to Sara's work place and tell her his love directly. But before going there he wanted to be sure that she was there at that time. To be more cautious, he decided not to call from the home telephone line. He knew that if he used a cell phone, his number would be displayed on the monitor of the telephone which he had called. So the best and most secure way was using an internet telephone system or voip. He had installed the required software long time ago. He closed the door of his room and picked up his laptop and went to the farthest part of the room and after setting the microphone to the laptop and entering the voip system, he started dialing. First he called the telephone directory and got the telephone number of the company in which Sara worked. Then he dialed one of the numbers that he got from the telephone directory and asked that when the employees of that company would leave .He understood that the employees of the accountancy department worked until 1:30 p.m. Then he told the person who was on the phone that he wanted to talk to one of the employees, whose name was Sara Warner. Roy heard Sara's voice just five seconds later. "Hello, I'm Sara Warner." Roy lost his head once he heard Sara's voice and couldn't say anything and cut off the phone. But at least he could rest assured that Sara was at work at that time and he also knew the time when she would leave. It was 11:30 and it was almost along time to 1:30. He did not change his clothes and told Kathryn that he wanted to go to some of his friends for a research work in order to do his research with help of them. He knew that lying was not good especially to his mother whom Roy loved from the bottom of his heart. But he had to be cautious. Roy said to himself, "I'll go to her company and will wait until she comes out Then I will tell her that I love her.

Maybe she'll love me, too and maybe she'll oppose to my feeling. In the first case, I will marry her and if the second one happens, I will forget her forever." Roy didn't try to show himself differently. He went out of home with his usual clothes and hair style. At first he decided to go by bicycle, but when he thought about the relatively too long distance between his house and Sara's work place, he changed his mind and went there by metro. On the way to go to his love's work place in order to express his love to her, Roy couldn't believe that it was he himself who was going there. But when he thought that sooner or later he should marry, he became more confident. He should give up fear and shame. He knew that he should express his love to Sara before it was going late, otherwise he may blame himself forever. And if he suppressed his feelings because of fear and shame, he may become disillusioned forever. He didn't have any fear and believed that it was completely true to do that work. The metro would arrive at the station up to a few minutes which was too close to Sara's work place. After the metro stopped at the station,

Roy detrained and went out of there. He had to walk for some minutes to get there. It was 12:15 and he had still much time. So he decided to go on foot. He almost knew all parts of the city and he didn't have any problem in finding the address. After 20 minutes walk, he got to the company in which Sara worked. It was obvious from the large building of the company that it was a large company. That company worked in packing the materials. It was still around an hour to the time when Sara finished her work and this made him more relax. The company building had ten floors and an open vast area which seemed to be used as a parking. The company's area was open to public and Roy waited there for about half an hour and decided to remain there until Sara went out. But being a large company and hiving a lot of employees made Roy be uncertain. He thought about this issue that maybe he couldn't find Sara among the other employees. So he decided to enter the building. First he asked one of the building's guards the exact address of the rooms related to the accountancy part and the guard guided him. Then he went to the accountancy department which was on the first floor. Roy understood quickly from the small boards of each room that three rooms were related to the accountancy part of the company. Those rooms placed in the same row. He just passed them. When he was passing the second room, he saw Sara was working. Roy saw her in a moment and immediately recognized her. Sara's look was downward that she was writing something in the file in front of her. She didn't see Roy in the corridor opposite to her room. Roy was anxious again. He didn't know what to do. He tried so much to overcome his fear and anxiety and entered Sara's room, but he couldn't. Then he went away from her room, and stood at the end of the corridor. He was waiting for Sara impatiently. He remained there until Sara came out. It was 1:30. Sara and her cooperators were going out of their rooms. Roy went a bit farther and stood in another corridor which was in front of the exit door. He was so careful. He followed Sara to the street opposite to the company secretly. Sara stood at the side of the street. It appeared that she wanted to take a taxi. Roy thought with himself that it was the best opportunity to talk to Sara, so he gave up fear and went to her. "Hello, Miss. Warner." "Hi, I guess you are my brother's friend, Roy. What are you doing here?" said Sara after a slight hesitation. "Well, I'm here to tell you something," said Roy. In these moments speaking was more difficult for Roy. However, he didn't want to hide the truth and made all of his effort to express his feelings toward Sara. "Well, to tell you the truth, I love you," said Roy. "What?!... You love me?!" said Sara surprisingly. "I tried so much to forget you, but I couldn't. Do you love me, too?" said Roy. "Truly speaking, I like you, too, but don't you think that we should speak to each other more?" said Sara. Roy, who became so happy, said, "Yes, you're right. What do you think about going to a restaurant and have lunch there?" "I agree," said Sara. Then they went to a restaurant on the other side of the street and after ordering the food, they started speaking. They asked a lot of questions from each other, that they became more confident by hearing the answer of each question. They decided to have relationship with each other just as two friends and hide their love from their parents for a couple of weeks or if necessary up to several months, and wait for some time to be acquainted with each other more. However, Sara asked Roy to tell David about his love and she was not agreed to hide this from David. And Roy said that although it was difficult for him, he would tell David about this matter on that day. Then both of them returned home. Roy was so happy. When he got home, he soon came to his room and lay on his bed to rest. He thought about the day he had spent and still couldn't believe he heard the sentence "I like you, too" from Sara, his favorite girl. But there remained another problem; he had to tell David that he loved Sara. Although he didn't worry about this so much because Sara herself was important and she loved Roy, too, he felt a little worried. He thought maybe David would be disagreed with his marriage with Sara. After he knew that Sara loved him, too, he became so happy that he felt each cell of his body was full of energy and comfort. Roy went to David in the afternoon. David first thought that Roy came to him for chatting, but after a while he understood that he was wrong. When Roy wanted to tell David that matter, he felt anxious. It was a hard time. David was Roy's best and most intimate friend. If David did not agree with this marriage, it certainly would affect their friendship negatively and may disrupt their close relationships. But it seemed that day was one of Roy's best days of life. Not only David did not disagree with Roy and Sara marriage, but also he became so happy and even told Roy that why he didn't tell him about this matter first. Then Roy and David decided to go to a game net which was only 50 meters far from David's home. They played for 45 minutes. When Roy returned home, he studied his lessons for about an hour. He was full of energy and motivation. He could achieve one of his most important goals of life. Sara was the only girl that Roy loved. Roy's energy for doing his daily works increased a lot. He didn't lose his concentration while studying and it was interesting that his concentration for study had increased much more than before. Loving Sara gave him energy and motivation like a strong engine. He was deep in studying and reviewing his lessons that Kathryn came to his room and said that Kathy Johnson was on the phone and wanted to talk to him. "Hello," said Roy. "Hello, Roy. This is Kathy. How are you?" said Kathy. "Fine and you?" said Roy. "I'm fine, too, I call you to remind you our appointment at 5 o'clock," said Kathy. "I don't forget. I'll be in the exhibition at 5:00," said Roy. "I'll see you," said Kathy. "Thanks for your call bye," said Roy. "Bye," said Kathy. Then Roy took the wireless phone to the living room and put it there and returned to his room. Roy had good feelings toward Kathy and she was his most intimate friend after David. Roy's happiness increased after Kathy's call. In a moment Roy looked at the necklace which his grandpa had given him. Roy was so busy that he forgot grandpa's gift totally. The reflection of the light which shone from the environment on the necklace made it more beautiful that it was simply recognizable on the wall from a far distance. Roy intended to wear the necklace for going to the exhibition. Then in order not to forget it, immediately took it and put it around his neck. It seemed that its green side was more beautiful than the blue one. He took a look at himself in the mirror. The necklace was more beautiful than Roy thought. As if a green eye was on his chest. Roy decided to put the necklace on his neck forever. He thought with himself that in this case he would enjoy the beauty of necklace and also whenever he looked at it, he would remind his grandpa and he never would forget him. Roy was not a person who did show off with his clothes or attract others. So he concealed the necklace under his shirt. It was 4 o'clock in the afternoon and he was ready to go to the exhibition. The clothes which he had chosen to wear weren't his usual clothes. He usually wore suit for going to the university or going out, but on that day he decided to go differently. He wore a white t-shirt and blue jeans and sport shoes. He got to the exhibition at 4:40 while he should have been there on 5:00. Roy got there 20 minutes earlier than his appointment with Kathy. He wandered around the exhibition. There were not many people there. He was seeking Kathy, but she had not come yet. So he didn't seek her anymore and decided to watch the paintings. In order to be protected from any damages, each of the paintings was placed in an anti-bullet and antiknock glass container. Roy was at the end of the saloon and decided to start watching the paintings from there. He gazed at a painting and suddenly he understood that he was in a room which was completely different from the environment of the exhibition. A man with a relatively strange and classic appearance and old clothes was standing exactly in front of him. He held a paintbrush in one hand and a circle plate on which oil colors were placed on the other hand. Although there wasn't any lamp in the room, the environment of the room was completely light because of the lights which entered from the window. That man became more surprised than Roy. The man said while he was surprised of Roy's existence in that room and his appearance, "oh, my God. Who are you?! What are you doing here?! How queer appearance you have!" Roy said, "Can you explain these circumstances? Is it a hidden camera? Where is here? "This time the man said with a British accent, "This is my house. It seems that you are British, but your accent is a little different from British." "Oh, no man. I'm American," said Roy. "America, where is America? I haven't heard this word yet," said the man. Then the man took the painting which was on a canvass in front of him and it s wet colors showed that it was painted recently. Once the man took the painting, Roy said, "oh, my goodness, don't touch it. You know if you damage the painting, what a penalty you should pay?" The man didn't pay any attention to Roy's words and hung the painting on the wall. "Can you tell me where is here?" asked Roy. "This is Florence," said the man. Roy said while laughing at man's words, "Florence?!..." And the man replied, "Yes, Florence. Don't you hear this name? Do you know where Italy is?" Roy said again while laughing, "No, you just know where Italy is." Then he became more serious and said, "Here is New York." Then he thought about the man's words and wandered around the house. He understood that the environment of that house was completely different from the exhibition. Then Roy asked the man whether he could know his name. The man said, "I'm Leonardo daVinci." Roy started laughing again and said, "Well, I'm Albert Einstein. Nice to meet you." This time Leonardo became more serious and said, "I don't know where you come from, but in our land when someone wants to go to another person's house, he will first knock on the door. Maybe you are a magician that suddenly appeared at the back of me." By hearing the word magician Roy suddenly remembered the necklace on his neck. Because grandpa had told him that it was magical. It was hard for Roy to believe it. He went toward Leonardo daVinci. I don't know how I entered this house, but I think all of these problems are related to this necklace. Then while Roy was talking to daVinci, all of a sudden both of them understood that they were not at that house, but at the exhibition. Roy didn't know what was happened. Roy took a look at his watch. It was still 4:40. Roy looked at the necklace again. The green side was on the back and the blue side was on the front. Roy, who was puzzled and a little frightened, decided to leave the exhibition before Kathy reached there. But the thing which was so strange was that some of the paintings were not in their places. It means that some of the glass containers became empty while there were some pictures in them a few minutes ago. Roy became completely confused. DaVinci was still perplexed and shocked. He was a little uncomfortable. Roy decided to leave the exhibition together with the man who called himself daVinci as quickly as possible. So he held daVinci's hand and persuaded him to go with him out of the exhibition. After exiting the exhibition, they went a little farther. Roy felt that he had fallen in trouble. Both of them were frightened a lot. Roy said, "See, Man! I don't know who are you, but I think that both of us are fallen in a big trouble. Will you tell me the truth if I ask you a question?" "Yes, of course," replied daVinci "what is your real name?" asked Roy. "Leonardo daVinci, what is your real name?" said the man. "I'm Roy Smith," said Roy. "Where is here? Why am I here now?" asked daVinci. "The name of this city is New York and the name of this country is America or it's better to say United States," replied

Roy. "I haven't heard the name of this country yet," said daVinci. "You're right because in the Middle Ages the continent of America and the country of America were not discovered. This country was made by the migrant people who had migrated from England to this land and it gradually developed and changed to this present America. We are now in the 21 century and the year 2006. DaVinci said, "See Mr. Smith I don't know how you brought me to this land, but I think you must be a magician." "No, I'm not a magician. I'll explain everything for you. I'm not a magician, but I'm sure that this necklace, which is around my neck, is magical. And in order to stop these troubles, I will took off this necklace and put it in my pocket," said Roy. "Oh, my God. I can not believe it. I was at home and deep in painting. By just then I finished that painting, Roy Smith turned up and brought me here," said daVinci. Roy, who really was sure that he was Leonardo daVinci, said, "Mr. DaVinci! I'm so sorry, it was my fault, but I promise that everything will turn as before. Believe me that I didn't do it on purpose. Everything was happened by accident." "You can not return me to my land and my house right now," said daVinci. "I know that it's difficult for you to believe, but truly speaking I still don't know how I should do this. I need some time. Please be more relax. I know that accepting these circumstances is difficult for you, but now you are in the 21 century and the year 2006 or simply speaking you are not living in the middle ages anymore," said Roy. "By middle ages you mean sixteenth century?" asked daVinci. "Forgive me. I didn't remember that you didn't call those years middle ages," said Roy. "But now what should I do? If you are right and everything happened by accident, what should we do right now? Do something, Mr. Smith," said daVinci. "There is a solution certainly. So don't worry. Besides, it's better to call me Roy instead of Mr. Smith," said Roy. "You can call me Leonardo instead of Mr. daVinci," said daVinic. "Well, Leonardo. We should be together for a couple of days and think well in order to find a good solution. First you should change your clothes," said Roy. "What's wrong with my clothes?" daVinci said surprisingly. While they were walking slowly on the street, continued speaking with each other. Most of the people who passed by their side laughed at daVinci's clothes. "See Leonardo there is nothing wrong with your clothes, but if you want to remain in this city, you should wear clothes like the people of this city. Other wise the people will laugh at you and ridicule you," said Roy. DaVinci said after he thought for a while, "okay." "Another problem is related to your name. You should change your name temporarily. If you tell the others that you are Leonardo daVinci, they will certainly think that you are crazy, and you may fall in trouble," said Roy. "Oh, no Roy! I can not accept to change my name." said daVinci. "Trust me Leonardo, it's for a short time," said Roy. DaVinci who couldn't accept to change his name said seriously, "I can not change my name." "Okay, if you don't believe me and don't want to change your name, it's better to try it right now and you'll see that I'm not kidding. For example tell your name to some of these people around us," said Roy. DaVinci went farther from Roy seriously and said to an elderly man who was walking on the pavement, "Hello, Mr.! I'm Leonardo daVinci. Can you tell me that where is here?" Then that man looked at daVinci with sympathy and said, "oh, my God! See what did life pressures do on this man. Take it easy man! Life is not so difficult that you imagine." DaVinci, who did not want to pay attention to that elderly man's words, went to another passerby who was a young girl and said, "I'm Leonardo daVinci. Can you tell me where is here?" That girl who had heard these words started laughing and said, "Is it hidden camera? How funny clothes you wear." DaVinci, who did not want to believe Roy, went to another passerby and said, "I'm Leonardo daVinci. What is the name of your land?" That man who was a teenager boy said, "I think you are afflicted with schizophrenia, a serious type of it, I almost know something about the symptoms of this disease. You should go to a psychological hospital as soon as possible. Maybe there is a hope for your recovery." DaVinci, who understood that Roy was right, went to Roy again and said, "Okay Roy. I will change my name, too. But before that, can you explain a bit about the sentences that they had told me? Why did they treat with me like this? Are my words ridiculous?" "No, not at all. But now you should change your clothes. I'll explain everything for you later. Move Leonardo, do not stop, come with me!" said Roy. They started walking again. "First, I should find a good name for you. Let me think ... John for your first name and walker for your last name. Great! From now you are John walker. I'll call you John," said Roy. After they walked a little forward, they arrived at a clothing store. "Hi, I want to buy a set of suitable clothes for my friend next to me," said Roy. "Are you making a television program?" said the seller. "So what?" said Roy. "It's obvious from your friend's appearance that you were making a TV program," said the seller. "What is he talking about, Roy? What does he mean?" asked daVinci. "Don't worry, John! I'll explain for him. We were engaged in making a TV program, like the hidden camera programmes. But our program is so funny and is different from the other hidden cameras," said Roy. "On which channel it will be displayed?" asked the seller. "On channel 8. After recording some sequences , John , our first player , understood that his real clothes were lost and now he asked us to buy him a set of clothes like those one and if he returns home with , different clothes , he may have problem with his wife , because they were John's wedding clothes," said Roy . "Oh, I see," said the seller. Then they chose a set of suit after trying some sets of black suits. They also bought a white shirt and a grey tie. "You are really hand some man! Now we should just think about your shoes," said Roy. Then they went to a shoe store beside the clothing store and bought a pair of black leather shoes. Afterwards they went out of there and continued walking again, but this time they did not walk without purpose, they moved toward the nearest metro station. "Very well John! Now It's better," said Roy. "Can you explain for me that what is TV program or hidden camera? Up to now I have heard these words from you and the people of this city, specially "hidden camera," said daVinci. "Well, you know, maybe it's difficult to explain it for you. But hidden camera is a kind of comic program that a person pull others leg for kidding and laughing in order to see their reflections. Those scenes are recorded by a camera and are shown on TV and all of the people can watch those scenes and will laugh and amuse. Hidden camera is in fact a kind of comic program for making people laugh that in our time it has a lot of fans and most of the people like these programmes. Because of this fact some people thought that we were recording hidden camera program. Your clothes were a little unusual and funny and all of the people thought that we were pulling their legs. Do you know what I mean?" said Roy. "I got the things that you said about making a comic program and hidden camera, but how is it possible for all people to watch that program? What do you mean by "television?" said daVinci. "See John! First of all their image is recorded by a camera on a video tape, then this video tape is sent to a TV network, after wards While the film is broadcasting, the waves will be sent from a transmitter to a satellite .These waves will be sent by a satellite to all over the world and it's possible to get the images by a satellite receiver in every part of the world. That is, a program is showing on TV at a particular time for all people around the world .Of course some of the networks are cable and for receiving them we need no satellite dish," said Roy.

"I don't get what you mean, Roy!" said daVinci. "It's not important. When you see the television and work with it, you'll understand what I mean. Now we will go home. I mean my home. Don't worry about our home. You can stay with us until you like. The only thing is that you don't have an identification card. Of course if you are careful, nothing bad will happen. But you should be careful not to be seized by police; otherwise you will fall in a big trouble because you don't have an identification card. "What is an identification card?" asked daVinci. "Today's life is too different from the life of hundreds years ago. Anyone who wants to live in a country must have nationality and identification card. Since you aren't American and don't have an identification card, police will seize you and imprison you for illegal immigration if it reveals that you don't have an identification card." "Prison!" said daVinci. "Don't fear man! I just told you these to be more careful. If you are careful, nothing bad will happen. I know that it's difficult for you to believe, but this happened and now you are at our time. We need some time to think about these problems and solve it," said Roy. "But what if our thinking won't be effective?" "We will certainly find a solution. Don't worry. Imagine that you are traveling for several days," said Roy. Then they arrived at the metro station. "Try not to ask me a lot on the train. Because some people may ridicule us again," said Roy. "But why?" asked daVinci. "When we get home, I'll answer all of your questions. Just try not to ask me a lot on the train because your answers are too simple for public that they think you are crazy," said Roy. "Okay, but before we get on the train can I ask you another question?" said daVinci. "Yes, ask, " replied Roy. "Why the wagons of here are so queer? Why they don't have any horses?" asked daVinci. "See, they aren't wagons. They are a little similar to wagon, but they don't have any horses. They are one kind of transporting vehicles, but instead of horses they use motors. Well it's a little complex and time-consuming to explain it. If I want to explain it for you now it will take a long time. The train comes, let's get on." After they entered the train and sat, Roy brought out his mp 3 player which was able to play video files from his pocket and turned it on then he put one of the headphones in daVinci's ear and the other one in his ear. Soon after the first video clip was played daVinci said surprisingly, "can you tell me how did you put that man in this box?" Roy said slowly, "No John, this is not a real man. This is just his picture and this is only a music player." DaVinci said, "Maybe you are really a magician! Don't you want to imprison me like him?" "Oh, no. Believe me it's just a player. If I had imprisoned him, he would have told you. He is not real. This is just a film," said Roy. DaVinci didn't say anything as if he was persuaded a little. Roy changed that music and played another audio music. "Are all of these sounds come from this small box?" asked daVinci. "Yeah, I put all of these musics in this box and now I can choose each of them that I like and will listen to it," replied Roy. "What a strange box it is!" said daVinci. "See John! For changing the music you should just press this button. This button plays the next music and this one plays the previous music." DaVinci held that on his hands and looked at it carefully as if he became interested in that music player. Then he pressed the music changer buttons and changed the music several times. "Can you explain for me that how these men with different instruments are in this small box?" asked daVinci. "You're making a mistake, John! There isn't anyone in this box. You just hear their voice which is recorded before," replied Roy. DaVinci didn't ask Roy anything else up to the end of the route. Then they detrained. "Can you tell me why you move under the ground instead of on the ground?" asked daVinci. "Well, it's too simple, be cause of the heavy traffic and also crowded streets, moving under the ground is the best and fastest way," replied Roy. "When we finally will arrive at your home?" asked daVinci. "We are near my house. Do you see that house there is a white car in front of it? The one which has blue bars on its walls," said Roy. "Yes, I am seeing it," said daVinci. "That is our house. When we enter the home you don't need to say anything to my parents. I'll explain everything for them," said Roy. "Okay, I won't say anything." They were 30 meters far from the house that suddenly daVinci saw a big airliner in the sky."What is that big bird with a horrible sound?" asked daVinci. "You mean an aero plane?" "This is another kind of transportation vehicle which moves in the sky instead of on the ground or under the ground. In fact it flies. I'll explain everything for you about the aero plane," said Roy. "You mean that there are a number of people in this vehicle?" "Yes, there are a lot of people in that aero plane. There are about 400 people in each of these airplanes that two individuals of them are pilot and a number of them are flight attendant and the others are passenger," said Roy. "Con you get me on that flying machine?" asked daVinci. "Yes, but not now. By the way its name is aero plane not flying machine," said Roy. They got home. "Hi Mom, Hi Dad! This is John Walker. One of my intimate friends and of course one of the university researchers who has helped me a lot yet," said Roy. Roy's parents greeted with daVinci and then they went to the living room. Roy asked his parents to go out of there for a moment and told them that there was an important issue he must tell them. Roy and his parents went to a room opposite to the living room in order to speak privately. Roy told his parents that Mr. Walker is one of the most important researchers of the university and he lost his memory in an accident because of a nervous shock and he even can not remember his family. And his doctor prescribed him to spend a couple of weeks with his colleagues or friends for his treatment. Roy also told his parents that Mr. Walker helped him a lot in research projects and in learning the lessons in past. Roy's parents accepted his words and told him that Mr. Walker could stay at their house until it was necessary. Then three of them returned to the living room. Roy turned on the TV. "Who's that person standing in this box, Roy?" asked daVinci. Roy looked at his parents and said, "Mom, Dad, you remember what I told you? This behavior is natural for him." Then Kathryn and Steven said, "Yes, we know what you mean." Afterwards Steven said, "There isn't any one in that box, Mr. Walker. This is just his image. By the way it's not a box, it's a television." Then Steven told daVinci that there were a number of empty rooms in their house and he could stay in which of them that he liked. Roy was talking when the telephone rang. Roy who couldn't he in the exhibition in due time, knew that Kathy was probably on the phone. Soon after the first ringing, Roy said, "I'll answer." Then he picked up the phone. It was Kathy. She asked Roy why he didn't go to the exhibition. Roy told her that one of his friends had an accident and he couldn't come. He also apologized Kathy for not coming there and Kathy told him that she was just worried about him. After he cut off, his parents asked him whom he talked to and he didn't say it was Kathy. He just told them that he had talked to one of his friends. "Dad, I think the room which is opposite to my room is the best for Mr. Walker," said Roy. Steven agreed with him and Roy took daVinci to his room. When they entered the room, Roy closed the door and said slowly, "I hope you forgive me that I call you John walker repeatedly." "Not important," said daVinci. "Now we should think well to find a way to return you to your time," said Roy. "I'm totally agreed with you, but can you explain how you suddenly entered my house?" said daVinci. "I had to be present in the exhibition at 5:00. Let me explain it for you from the beginning. From yesterday an exhibition of your paintings has been held in our city. I should tell you that your paintings are among the most expensive and attractive works of universe. One of my friends, Kathy, had bought a ticket for me and we made an appointment at 5:00 p.m to meet each other in the exhibition and watch the paintings. But I got there 20 minutes earlier, and I decided to wander around the exhibition. When I gazed at one of the paintings, suddenly I understood that I was at your house. But an important point is that at a time I gazed at your painting, I put on a necklace, which is my grandpa's gift, around my neck. I think all of these problems are due to that necklace. Because my grandpa told me that when he wanted to buy this necklace, its owner had told him that it was a magical necklace. Now we should think well and understand how this necklace works. But we should be too careful and we shouldn't act hurriedly. Otherwise we may face other problems." "Yes, you're right. We should think well to find a good solution. By the way would you please give me that necklace which is your grandpa's gift for a while?" said daVinci. "Okay, but don't put it around your neck," said Roy. "Okay," said daVinci. Then Roy brought out the necklace from his trousers' pocket and gave it to daVinci. daVinci looked at it for a while and delivered it to Roy again . "It's better to change your clothes, John! You don't need to wear these clothes at home. Well, I have a lot of clothes. You can wear some of my clothes," said Roy. Then Roy gave some of his clothes which he usually wore at home to daVinci and left him alone in the room to change his clothes. He himself went to the empty room in which daVinci was due to live and changed his clothes and returned to his room. "It's better, isn't it? You feel more comfortable," said Roy. "By the way, Roy! What was that tool that you put on your ear after it rang?" said daVinci. "This is telephone. People communicate with each other by this instrument. There is a telephone in every house and each telephone has a number and if someone dials a telephone number of someone else, he can talk to that person," said Roy. "Even if they are too far from each other?" said daVinci. "Yes," said Roy. A big monitor which Roy used as his computer monitor was in fact a plasma television that could be set on the computer. Roy most often used it as a television. Roy turned on the TV and said to daVinci, "see John! This is a television. It exists in different size and form. It's easy to work with this. You should just set the channels before. Then you hold this control in your hands and change the channels and choose your favorite channel. By these two buttons, you can change the channels and by these buttons beside them you can make the volume high and low. This red button turns off the TV .Now hold this in your hands. Press the red button. It turns off. Now press that button again. It turns on again. Well, now press one of those buttons which I told you change the channels. See how easy it is. You can simply work with television," said Roy. "Yes, that's right. I think I learn how to work with television," said daVinci. DaVinci changed the channel. The announcer of that network was reporting important news. "Now, don't change the channel for a moment," said Roy .The reporter was speaking about daVinci's paintings exhibition. The news was that some of the paintings were missed while the authorities of the exhibition do not have any evidence from the robbers, and even they don't know how the paintings were stolen. Neither the burglar alarm rang nor any thing Suspicious was seen in the exhibition. The reporter claimed that any image was not recorded by closed circuit cameras showing that the paintings were stolen from the exhibition. While closed circuit cameras indicate that the paintings were in their places at the early times of exhibition and they disappeared in less than one second. Another thing which made the reporter surprised was that why the robbers just stole a number of the paintings and why these robbers, who had stolen almost half of the painting skillfully and without leaving any evidence, did not steal all of the paintings. This report indicated clearly that everybody was shocked   of this robbery. "Oh, my God. What a trouble! Almost half of the paintings were stolen," said Roy. DaVinci started changing the channels again. Roy, who became anxious after hearing that news, was walking in the room and thinking. He continued this work for almost 10 minutes. Suddenly he said, "I get it, John! Those paintings are not stolen. They're disappeared. Because they belong to the time when you are not at. You know what I mean?" "No, can you explain more clearly?" said daVinci. "See, those paintings which are now in the exhibition belong to the time before you come here and those which are disappeared belong to the time after you come to our time and now because you are at our time they are disappeared. Now you see what I mean?" said Roy. "Yes, exactly," said daVinci. "Oh, my God. All of these disorders and problems are my fault. How can I compensate for all of these losses?" said Roy. "Don't worry boy! We will certainly find a solution," said daVinci. "The only way to compensate for this loss is to return you to your time. Now how can I compensate for these losses; while I don't know how can I return you to your time?" said Roy. "As I understood from that report those paintings must be too expensive. Now are they know that you cause them to disappear?" said daVinci. "No, we are luck or it's better to say I am lucky that they don't have any evidences from us." "Be hopeful, boy! We'll succeed." DaVinci was watching TV when a program about aero planes showed on TV. DaVinci was watching that program with a special excitement. It was obvious from his face that he had a special interest in flying. He told Roy, "Is it that flying machine which we saw in the sky when we wanted to go home?" "This is an aero plane, too. But it's different from the one that we saw. There are millions of aero planes in all over the world that they in crease every day." "How this thing works?" "Well, it's a little difficult to explain, but I'll try to say it in a way that you can understand. Each aero plane consists of a one or more engine and a fuselage. The body of an aero plane is made of light, resistant and hard materials and the most important factor which causes an aero plane to fly is its aerodynamic body." Then he picked up a paper and pen and drew a thing. "Being aerodynamic means that the surfaces under the body and wings of the aero plane are completely flat and smooth and on the body and wings are a little curved. So the air pressure under the aero plane exceeds the air pressure above the aero plane and the aero plane can fly and remain in the sky. But the factor which causes an aero plane to move is its engine. The engine of an aero plane is usually jet that provides the required force of moving and in fact pushing the aero plane forward," said Roy. "Can you get me on one aero plane?" asked daVinci. "Of course, I can, but there are some requirements. Flying has various types and aero planes are also various. If you want to get on an air liner, it will be a little difficult because you must have an identification card that unfortunately you don't have," said Roy. "When are we going to fly?" asked daVinci. "Tomorrow afternoon," replied Roy. "Can't we fly tomorrow morning?" asked daVinci. "No, I should go to the university tomorrow morning." said Roy. Roy was talking with daVinci that his cell phone rang. The number which was displayed on his phone was David's number. "Hello," said Roy. "Hello," said Sara. "Is this you, Sara?" said Roy. "Yes, How are you, Roy?" "Fine, are you okay?" "Yes, are you free tomorrow noon?" "Yeah, but I'll have class until 10:30." "I will come at 10:30 to go out with each other." "Okay, that's good. I will wait for you in the third floor, in front of the room number 52." "Okay, I will remember."

"By the way, where we gonna go?" asked Roy." We will go to Lotus restaurant tomorrow noon," said Sara. "I will go if I myself pay the bill," said Roy." Well if you, it won't account as my invitation," said Sara. "Okay, we'll talk about it later. By the way, how did you find my cell phone number?" said Roy." I took it from David," said Sara. Roy seemed a little nervous. When he was talking to Sara, he felt that his tongue was locked and his mind couldn't combine the words well and made a sentence. Finally, Roy said the last sentences of his conversation with Sara and cut off the phone. "I love you," said Roy." Me too," said Sara. "Bye," said Roy. "Good bye," said Sara." Is the thing which you hold in your hand a telephone, too?" asked daVinci." Yeah, but you can carry it everywhere," said Roy. "Was the person whom you were talking with your wife?" asked daVinci. "No. she is my fiancée," said Roy. "Do you love her so much?" asked daVinci. "Yes," replied Roy. "It was obvious from your way of speaking and your face that she is very important for you and you love her so much," said daVinci. "There is just one problem," said Roy." What problem?" "My parents don't know that we are engaged. Don't say anything about this to them. I don't want them to know this matter now." "Okay, I won't say anything." "By the way, I hope you didn't be offended that I called you with your unreal name. Because now I 'm completely aware and believe who you are." "I don't mind." Then Roy removed the cable of television's antenna from the plasma monitor and connected the cable of computer's monitor to it in order to use it as a monitor for his computer. And then he turned on the computer and started playing. He was playing an action game that suddenly daVinci became angry and said to Roy, "Oh, no! You killed that person." Roy, who became surprised at daVinci's sudden reaction, said, "No, I didn't kill him. It was just a game. They are not real, John! They are just like the humans." "But you kill some people just now." "It works like the television. You know it's not real. Try it and see that it's just a game." DaVinci, who was convinced a little, said, "Well, what is this game in which people should be killed?" Roy talked to him more that finally he could persuade him that it was just a computer game, not a real war. Then Roy gave the joystick to daVinci and asked him to play. DaVinci shot a little and said, "It is more interesting than it seems. It's enjoyable." "You see, man! It's just an unreal war. It's like that you want to practice shooting." "Yes, I know what you mean." After some minutes Roy exit that game and started another game. DaVinci liked that game more because it had more vehicles and varied environment. "Roy! I really like to get on those strange drays." "They are not drays, they are automobiles." The style of that game was in a way that most of its stages were related to the automobile. DaVinci enjoyed driving the automobiles, although they weren't real. They played for almost two hours. Then they exit that game and turned off the computer. "It was very interesting and amusing. By the way, you said what the name of this was?" "Computer" "It was very attractive. As if I were really in that dray and I drove it." "No, don't say dray, it's an automobile." "Yes, automobile. By the way if I ask you to do something for me right now, can you do it?" "What should I do?" "When we were entering your house, I saw an automobile in your yard. Would you please get me in it? I mean will you take me to the street by that automobile?" "No, not now, because it's 10 o' clock at night. Besides I don't have a driving license." "What is a driving license?"

"It's a kind of card that having it means a permit for driving. If a person drives without having a driving license, police will arrest him and also his car." "Can't we drive the car tonight?" "It's not my car; it is my father's automobile. Besides, since my father knows that I don't have a driving license, he won't let me drive his car." DaVinci went farther as if he was offended by Roy's reaction and said, "Okay, I don't want. You speak in a way that you have to do a hard task. Remember Roy that you are responsible for bringing me to your time." Roy hesitated for a moment and said happily, "I get it John. I get it. I will ask my father to lend me his car, but you should drive. I will tell him that you have a driving license. So he will surely agree." DaVinci said happily, "I knew that you would accept my request." Then Roy asked his father to lend him and daVinci his car for about thirty minutes and said to him that Mr. Walker had driving license. Steven accepted Roy's request, but he advised him to be careful. Dad was so tired that he wanted to go and sleep. After talking to Roy and giving him the switch of the car, he went to his room to sleep. But Kathryn accompanied him to the yard and asked him when they would come back. Roy said, "Don't worry, Mom! We just want to wander around the city and will come back soon." Then Roy got in the car and started in order to drive it to the street. When Roy sat in the car, his mother asked, "You said that Mr. Walker would drive, didn't you?"

"Yes, Mom! I just want to drive it out, and then we will change our sits."

"Okay, go." When Roy was driving the car out of the yard, Kathryn went into the house. Roy got out the car and closed the door of the yard. Then they went while daVinci sat on the front seat of the car next to Roy. "Hey, John! Did you understand how lucky we were?" said Roy. "No, what luck?" "I had told my parents that you lost your memory and you had a brain problem. Wow, man! We were lucky that they didn't remember you were sick; otherwise Dad would never land his car to us. Now I will take you to a big and quiet street that we can drive so fast and enjoy." Then they went to a relative quiet street of the city.

But Roy didn't dare to drive more than the speed of 100 kilometers per hour. He was too careful. He was aware that if anything bad happened, he himself and daVinci would get into trouble. Afterwards they went to one of the districts of the city. "Can I drive the car?" asked daVinci. "No, not now. I should first instruct you driving. You know if something happens to Dad's car or police arrest us, we will get into a big trouble," said Roy. "How pessimistic you are! If you are careful, nothing bad will happen." "You know where am I going now?" "No." "I am going to one of my old friend who is a professional in speed races. We will enjoy a lot tonight." It was 10:30 and about thirty minutes had passed from the time Roy went out. Then Roy stopped in front of a house. A boy opened the door. "Hi, Dennis!" "Hi, Roy!" Dennis and Roy hugged each other. "You make me so excited, boy! How did you suddenly remember me?" "I missed you so much." "Me, too." "By the way, Dennis! Are you still working in that car racing club?" "Yes." "Can you take us there tonight to drive fast with my friend?" "Yes, but you should finish soon. You know if my boss understands, I may get into trouble." "Don't worry, boy! We are careful." "By the way, Roy! There is still another thing that I should tell you." "What?" "I myself will drive until we get there." "Okay." "How great this car is! Is it yours?" "No, it's my father's car." "I guess it because you never like car racing." Then Dennis looked at the car again and said, "Oh, my God! I can't believe it!" "By the way, Dennis! This is John Walker, one of the researchers of our university." "Nice to meet you, Mr. Walker." "Nice to meet you, too." "Okay, its better to get in and go soon." Then they went toward the car racing club. "Roy! You and your friend are very lucky since tonight no practice race will be held on the piste. Tonight that is Wednesday nights are the only times of the week that the club or its better to say car racing piste is empty." "Would you please drive more slowly?" asked Roy. "I can't because it's one part of our term. Don't worry Roy! Nothing will happen to the car," replied Dennis. "How powerful this car is!"

"Oh, my God! The speed is near to 320 kilometers per hour. Look at the hand of the speedometer, Dennis! Drive slowly." " We just drive with this speed up to the end of this street; afterwards I will reduce the speed." And after 15 seconds Dennis reduced the speed and drove with usual speed. "How enjoyable it is!" said daVinci. At last they got at the piste. Dennis got out of the car and after greeting with the guard, they entered the piste by car. It was obvious from the way in which Dennis was talking to the guard that they knew each other well. Then Dennis got out of the car and Roy sat behind the steering wheel of the car again. Dennis advised him to be careful and then Roy started driving the car. While Roy was changing gear and speeding up, he said to daVinci, "Well, man! It's better to prepare yourself for a perfect excitement now." Roy changed gear so much that he got to sixth gear and then he pushed the auto accelerator. The path, which Roy was passing through, was completely straight and the road was without any turn up to almost one kilometer farther. The speed of the car was 360 kilometers per hour. Roy continued driving with this speed for just several seconds later and then reduced the speed because other parts of the piste were not straight and some parts had sharp turns. They drove with high speed for almost ten minutes. Although Roy's work was very dangerous, he did it very carefully and increased the speed of the car only on the straight roads which didn't have any turn. Both of them were full of excitement and joy. "Can I drive, too?" asked daVinci. "No, but I will reduce the speed and you can control the steering wheel." replied Roy. Roy reduced the speed of the car to 30 kilometers per hour and while he was completely careful, let daVinci control the steering wheel. "Be careful, John! As I explained for you, if you turn the steering wheel to the right, the car will go to the right and if you turn it to the left, it will go to the left," said Roy. After some minute daVinci said, "Now would you please hold it?" "Yes, I will hold it right now." said Roy. "Can you instruct me driving, Roy?" "Yes, but not now, because it takes along time and needs so much practice. Now its better to come back home, otherwise my parents will be worried," said Roy. And then they returned home after took Dennis home. After drinking some coups of tea, they started playing the computer games again and continued this task up to 11:30. Then both of them slept. Roy slept in his room and daVinci in the room in front of his room. Next day Roy talked to Kathy in the university before his class started and apologized for not going to the exhibition. But it seemed that Kathy was not mad with Roy so much. Kathy had the similar class. In class she sat beside Roy. It seemed that Kathy learned the lessons better than Roy. However, when Roy didn't understand something, Kathy helped him. Kathy took notes from all of the important points and materials. Roy had good feelings that Kathy was sitting next to him. Kathy wrote quickly the words of the professor and formulas and whatever written on the board and this was useful for Roy. Roy couldn't take notes as quickly as Kathy did. So he copied the notes of Kathy. Kathy was a kind and intimate friend for Roy and she also helped him in his lessons .When the class finished, Kathy went out with Roy. Sara was waiting in front of the class on time. Roy went to her and said, "Hi". "Hi," said Sara. Kathy joined them, too and greeted with Sara. "This is Kathy Johnson, one of my class mates," said Roy .Then he looked at Kathy and said, "This is Sara Warner. We are engaged to marry soon." Kathy asked hastily, "Are you engaged?" "Not yet, but we love each other .By the way, I forgot to say that she is David's sister," said Roy. Kathy asked Sara, "Are you a student?" "No, I' m the employee of NPC company," replied Sara. Roy said to Kathy, "I do not have any other classes today and Sara is free, too .We want to go to a restaurant with each other." "Oh I m sorry to take your time," said Kathy. Roy said with smile, "No, it s not important .You will be acquainted with my future wife more." Then Roy and Sara said good bay to Kathy and went out of the university .First they walked and talked with each other for about half an hour, then they took a taxi to lotus restaurant .As time passed, Roy felt that his love to Sara was increasing .Time passed slowly when he was with Sara. When they arrived at the restaurant and Roy remembered the moments that he spent at the university, it was like that he remembered several weeks ago .Love ,as a heavy weight, prevented the time to pass quickly and he felt that time passed so slowly like the early days that he fell in love with Sara .But this time loving Sara made him feel relaxed and not anxious or worried .Whenever Sara uttered the word "my dear" ,too much energy and happiness was created in Roy

.Although he seemed so relax and calm while talking to Sara ,he felt uneasy .He was so happy that he felt he wanted to fly .He felt lightness exactly like a paratrooper who was suspending in the sky, but he was on the ground. After they ate lunch at that restaurant, walked a little more and said good bye to each other and went .when Roy got home, Kathryn asked him why he came back late. Because he always came back home early on Thursdays and his mother knew well that he had just one class on Thursdays .She also asked him about not calling home and saying the reason of coming late .Roy did apologize for not calling Kathryn. It was obvious from the way Kathryn was speaking that she wasn't angry; however, she wasn't satisfied with Roy. "I forgot to call you and tell you I would come back late," said Roy. "Did you forget? Can you understand that how worried I was .I know that you are not a child, but you should under stand your parents. Remember that your parents always love you and worry about you," said Kathryn. "I' m sorry, Mom," said Roy. It s 1:30 pm now and you come home two hours late. I don't intend to blame   you, but please think about your parents a little .I was so worried about you," said Kathryn. "I promise not to do this again." said Roy. "Okay, I don' t mind. But next time you want to come back late, call me before that," said Kathryn. "okay," said Roy. Then Roy went to his room .He was a little upset that he made his mother worried, but loving Sara had created a very strong power in him to be happy and forget any upsets .He was still hearing Sara 's words as if she was there and talking to him. He was lying on his bed and rest .Thinking about Sara made him so busy that he forgot daVinci. He was listening to a joyful music and deep in his dreams. He felt drowsy and he wanted to sleep that suddenly he remembered daVinci .Where was he? From the time he entered home he didn't see him. He stood up rapidly and went to his room .A strange fear had surrounded him. He was afraid daVinci went out of the home. He was so anxious and worried that he opened the door with out knocking on it. DaVinci was lying on the bed .It was obvious from his face that he woke up just a few moments ago. "John, are you here?" asked Roy. "Yes," replied daVinci. "Oh, I· m sorry to wake you up you were sleeping," said Roy. "I don· t mind .By the way what did you do for flying?" asked daVinci. "Nothing, but don· t worry." Then Roy said more slowly, "let· s go to my room to tell you." When daVinci came to Roy's room, Roy felt more comfortable. It seemed that he didn't want his mother to hear his voice. "See John! This afternoon we will go to a company which works in the flying by kites. They rent and also sell the kites as well as instruct flying by kite." "Kite? What is a kite?" asked daVinci. "Well, maybe we can say that it's a type of airplane, but the very old one," said Roy. "No, I want to get on an airliner, from those I had seen on

TV," said daVinci. "It's not possible now. It needs some time .You don't have any identification card and you may get into trouble. But don t be upset. Many of the airplanes are easier to get on. Now I just can get you on a kite or a paraglide," said Roy. "What is a paraglide? What kind of plane is it?" asked daVinci. "Paraglide means an airplane without an engine. This kind of plane moves only by wind force. I know that flying by this aero plane can not satisfy you, but don't worry. You will fly. Be sure," said Roy. Then Roy's mother knocked on the door. "Roy! I bring your lunch." "Come in, mom!" Roy knew that if he told his mother that he had lunch before, she would be offended .So he took the lunch plate and thanked her. Then his mother went out of the room. "By the way, Roy! I learned how to work with TV, but I can't work with computer, I mean even I couldn't turn it on," said daVinci. "I will turn it on to play with each other," said Roy. Then he pressed the power key in order to turn it on and he started eating his lunch. He knew that if he didn't eat that food, his mother would certainly be offended. Roy loved his mother so much that he couldn't see his mother to be upset and annoyed .Although he wasn't hungry, he ate it and put its plate in the kitchen and then came back to his room. He started playing an action adventurous game with daVinci. DaVinci confronted with a new flying machine in that game. He saw a helicopter. That helicopter was one part of the stages of the game. DaVinci was interested in that part of the game. "What is this flying machine, Roy?" asked daVinci "This is a helicopter .Its structure is almost simple. Do you see that spinning blade on the surface of the   helicopter?" said Roy. "Yes, I see it," said daVinci. "The body of the helicopter can go straight up into the air with the help of that spinning blade which spins by the power of engine. Of course there is a smaller spinning blade at the end of helicopter's body or its tail which is used for the horizontal turning of the helicopter," said Roy. "Do we need an identification card for getting on a helicopter?" asked daVinci. "No" "So would you get me on the helicopter? It's not possible today." "Can we get on a helicopter instead of the kite?" "Well, Johan! Getting on a helicopter is not so easy that you think. Because the helicopter is an expensive vehicle and only specific people can use this vehicle .I mean rich and big shot people often get on this vehicle. Some of the helicopters are also related to governmental or military organizations that common people can not get on them." Roy became silent for a moment and thought a little. Then he stood up and said, "I get it, John!" Then he went toward his book shelf .He kept ancient history magazines in the bottom drawer of book shelf .Roy brought out a number of them and started searching quickly among them. He turned over the pages of the magazines quickly .He had seen an advertisement before which was related to a company that got the people on the helicopter and wandered them around the city .Roy searched a number of them that at last he found his intended advertisement .He detached that advertisement from the magazine and then went toward daVinci again and sat besides him. He didn't want his mother to be aware of his tasks since he couldn't bear her worry so he didn't use the telephone line of the home to call that company. He turned on his laptop computer and connected to the internet by wireless internet technology and then dialed the phone number of that company by voip technology and started talking .He asked several questions about the required cost and conditions of flying by the helicopters of that company .It was obvious from Roy's smile that he was satisfied with the answers which the secretary gave him and after getting his intended information, he cut off the phone. "John! You are going to get on a helicopter just today," said Roy. "Really?" "Yes, but you should accept a provision." "What is it? They want me to have an identification card, don't they?" Roy said with smile, "No, you should understand my conditions." And daVinci said with smile, "like what conditions..." "Well, see man! If everyday I want to get you on an aircraft after the university, no time will remain for me to study and do my daily tasks." " Do you mean that I bother you?" "Oh ,no .I didn't mean it .I mean if you want me to do something for you, give me a one or two-day chance and don't expect me to do it for you immediately." DaVinci said while laughing, "Yes, I know .It's again related to the identification card and these things." "No, I mean that you should be calmer." Then Roy exited that action adventurous game and they engaged in playing an automobile race game. DaVinci played with joystick and Roy with keyboard. They played for almost half an hour. Then Roy went to study his lessons, but daVinci continued playing. Roy studied for about one hour and then started playing the computer game again and after 30 minutes, he turned off the computer .He connected the TV's antenna cable to the plasma monitor and turned it on to watch TV. Missing daVinci's paintings was still one of the important news of the networks .After watching TV for about one hour ,Roy turned off the TV and said to daVinci, "It's better to go and change your clothes to go out." "Where are we going?" "Don't you want to get on a helicopter?" "Oh, now I get it." "Please be careful .If someone asks you who are you, you will say that you are John walker .If they also ask you to give them your identification card ,say that it is at home . Do you get it?" "Yes, I do. Don't worry." "Well, now go and change your clothes." And then both of them changed their clothes. "Roy! If I want you to do another work for me, will you accept it?" "Oh, my goodness! He starts his requests again. This time you certainly want to get on a shuttle, don't you?" "Can we go there by your father's car?" "Forget about it." DaVinci said with a kind and imploring face, "Roy! That's your father's car. You also know driving. So why we can not go by your father's car?" Roy said more slowly, "The problem is not just about driving the car. You know if the police become aware that we drive without having a driving license, what will happen next? Both of us will get in to trouble, man! Although your requests are very important for me, forget about this one please." "Well, how can they understand that you don't have a driving license?" "I know how you like getting in a car, but please understand me." DaVinci became annoyed a little and said, "I don't want to go by your father's car at all. Now do I understand you well?" Roy became silent for a while and said as if he found a good solution, "I find it .W e will go by my father's car." "But you said that we'll get into trouble," said daVinci. "Now I'll call David and ask him to drive. Because he has a driving license," said Roy. Then Roy picked up his cell phone and dialed David's number and told him that he himself would drive the car to his house and David should drive from there. Roy didn't say anything to David about the real identity of daVinci and just told him that he was one of the researchers of the university who was his friend. "John! He accepted my request. Now we should just ask permission from Dad to drive his car." They went to the living room to ask permission from Steven. Most often Steven was in the living room and he used to rest while watching TV. They entered the living room. Kathryn was also near Steven. "Dad! Would you please lend us your car for several hours?" asked Roy. "Yes, my son, but there is a problem," said Steven. "What problem?" asked Roy. Then Steven asked daVinci to go out for a moment as if he wanted to hide something from daVinci. Steven said while he spoke more slowly, "You don't have a driving license, Roy! We suppose that Mr. Walker has a driving license, but don't you say that he loses his memory and has a brain problem, so how can he drive?" "No, Dad! His amnesia is just related to his family members, living place and some of the scientific materials and he doesn't forget many other things such as, language, social behaviors, driving and so on. Dad! He is very important in our university. He is one of the most important researches of our university." "So why he didn't know what television is when you took him in our house?" "See Dad! I told you that he just lost a small portion of his memory and you shouldn't doubt about his psychological health. Trust me, dad!" And finally Steven let Roy take his car while it was obvious from his face that he wasn't completely convinced. "Roy! I hope you can understand why I'm strict about the car and I want you to know that this car is not worthy of you." Then Roy drove the car to the street and went to David with daVinci. They went there according to the address of that company and David would come there some hours later. They arrived at the company building. "John, watch it! Do you remember what I told you at home?" said Roy. "Yes, I do," said daVinci. "David! Please be careful a bout the car, otherwise I don't know how can I talk to my father." said Roy. "Don't worry boy! I, m careful," said David. "By the way, David! Please come and take us home at eight o'clock," said Roy. Then Roy and daVinci got off the car and entered the company building. The building of the company was a two –floor and relatively small building. They went to the area behind the building which was large and open after filling some forms and paying the flight cost. There were some helicopters on that ground and also several empty runways which were the landing place of other helicopters. One of the leaders took them to a helicopter and after checking their passes which the company had issued for them, he told the pilot to fly. Then the helicopter took off. "John! You know you should enjoy flying as much as you can since you can not fly with any kind of flying machine at least up to some weeks later," said Roy. "Why, Roy? Is there any problem?" asked daVinci. "No. I just pay almost all of my money for this flight. And I don't have any money up to one month later," said Roy. "By the way, Roy! You didn't bring any money with yourself so how did you pay the flight?" asked daVinci. "By my credit Card." said Roy. "What is a credit card?" "Don't confuse yourself. It's too simple. In fact, nowadays people use credit cards instead of money." "How do you put your money in this small and thin card?" "Forget about it. It's better to enjoy flying." "By the way, Roy! Why the buildings of your city are so tall and big?" "Because the population of the cities has increased so fast that they don't have enough capacity to construct more houses, so the buildings are made tall and vertical that more people can settle in them." "I understand what you mean, but how these tall and big buildings are constructed?" "By steel and concrete. First a metal skeleton of the building is made by steel pillars, and then the building is completed by concrete and brick." "Oh my goodness! I can not believe that I'm flying." "It's better to believe it because we are in the sky now." "Roy! I really thank you. I don't know if I didn't be acquainted with you, could I ever experience flying?" "It's not necessary to thank me. You came to our time just by accident and its main reason was that necklace which my grand father gave me. Hey, man! Look at that buildings and cars! Look at the people! Everything seems small from here." "Yes, from here cars, people and in general everything seems small." That helicopter wandered around the city for about one hour. When they got above the Liberty Statue, the helicopter turned around it in order to enjoy watching the statue more. "What a big statue is in your city!" said daVici. "Yes, its name is Liberty Statue. But we call it big apple," said Roy. "Who made this statue?" "This statue was made by Fredric Aguste Bartholdi, a French designer and sculptor. He was a genius. Look at the statue! See what a master piece he had created. This statue is not only big, but also very beautiful. Fredric had made this statue from 1875 to 1884 in France. This statue was carried to America by ship in 1885. Richard Dehunt started making its pedestals in 1877 and finally the statue was placed on the pedestals in 1886. This is the sign of liberty and democracy as well as its beauty. I have studied a lot of books about this statue." "This is really beautiful." And then the helicopter took them to the other parts of the city. This statue is a symbol of freedom and Humanity Rights. There are not Humanity rights and freedom in some countries. In USA everyone can choice his religion and his life style by himself and he is completely free to make decision and also he can say his political and religious or personal opinion freely. But in some countries like Iran and North Korea a lot of peoples are executed because of stating their different political and religious opinions.

Iran is one of the countries that there are a lot of restrictions are laid ahead of the youth. For example, a boy or a girl just due to loving each other's or a simple relationship will be whipped or detained. In Iran even the children bellow 18 are executed. And in Iran people cannot choose their religion and if they change or choose their religion they will be executed and in Iran and North Korea The life of millions of people depend on only one person who called leader and people in Iran and North Korea even cannot choice the style of their clothes or their hair dressing. But in USA there are some organizations that they defense the oppressed people. And then they saw the united nations building in New York.

This is the united nations building. All countries from all over the worlds have their representatives here. This institution established to make and keep the world peaceful and regulated. Some countries like USA always help to establish peace in all over the world and they fight against illegal and devastative activities. USA as a powerful and rich country in the world, is a symbol of democracy and freedom. USA and its allies always defend of and support innocent and oppressed people and they save them and bring their voice out and stand against ruthless countries and leaders (for example Iran), and make them to regard the international law and regulations.

At last it retuned at 7:55 to the area of the company. They went out of the company and went to the street opposite to the company. It was 8:00 and

David came there on time. They arrived home. "I really thank you, David. If I didn't have a friend like you, I don't know what could I do?" "Forget about it boy!" Then David said good bye to them in front of Roy's house and Roy parked the car in the yard. "Roy! Thank you," said John. "You're welcome," said Roy. Then they went to Roy's room and after changing their clothes, they started watching TV. "How can I get some painting instruments?" asked daVinci. "From a shop," said Roy. "How far is it from here?" "It's not important how far it is. Tomorrow I'll buy required things of painting for you when I want to come back home." Then they had dinner and after playing computer games for about one and half an hour, they slept. The next day Roy remembered flying with daVinci. Those scenes were showing before his eyes in the class. He felt that he didn't have enough concentration on the lessons. He was there physically, but not mentally. It seemed that experience made Roy to have different amusements. If that necklace was not given to him, he and daVinci would never meet each other and he would not experience flying by the helicopter. A great revolution was created in Roy, which cried loudly that he should enjoy his life more and not just think about his daily tasks. Roy spent most of the years of his life in the house and in his room. He seldom went on a trip and even when his parents traveled, he stayed home. He was so deep in these thoughts that he didn't pay any attention to the professor's speech and didn't understand anything. So after his class finished, Roy asked Kathy to give him her notes in order to take them home and copy them or scan them and save in his computer. Kathy's behavior was a bit strange on that day. She asked Roy about Sara several times and each time she asked a different question. Roy tried so much to change their subject of conversation, but he couldn't since Kathy again asked a question which led to Sara. Roy trusted Kathy and let her to ask him about his private life. Any how, Roy answered to Kathy's questions honestly and without any prejudice. On that day Roy didn't pay any attention to his class in the university and thought about daVinci until the last moments. He was conscience-stricken that he caused daVinci to come to his time. This made him to find a solution in order to improve these conditions. But his worry reached its climax when he felt weakness in returning daVinci to his time. Roy was so upset that his grandfather gave him that necklace. He steadily thought about this event and how these things happened. Any way, he couldn't do anything. He was aware that he should confront with these problems with patience and logic. That day on the way to come back home he seemed upset. But this didn't last for a long time. Because soon David started his jokes and Roy became livelier. In the middle of the way Roy told David that he wanted to get off the train in order to buy some painting instruments from a shop. He wanted to say goodbye to David, but David didn't accept that Roy went there alone. They got off the train and went to a shop near that station. "What do you want to buy that you get off the train?" asked David. "I want to buy some painting instrument," said Roy. "What? Painting? Do you paint?" said David. "No, but my friend, whom you acquainted with yesterday, I mean Mr. Walker, paints. Of course he paints for amusement and interest," said Roy. Roy bought some papers and also some oil color, but he didn't buy a tripod, painting canvas and brush because he had them at home. Roy liked painting several years ago, but this interest became lost gradually. The distance between the shop and subway station was too little and they got on the train after shopping when Roy got home, daVinci was watching TV. Roy went to his room after having lunch and drinking some coups of coffee. He lay on the bed. "By the way, Roy!

Today I could turn on the computer," said daVinci. "Really?" asked Roy. "Yeah." "Could you play, too?" "Yes. That's really great. You have a good progress." Although Roy felt tired, stood up and went toward davinci and sat next to him, behind the computer desk. "Well, please show me that," said Roy. "Okay, it's too easy. As you said I move that small sign on the monitor by this tool which you said is a mouse and then I take that sign on this picture and press my hand on the left side of the mouse. Now we enter the game," said daVinci. "It's too great, man! You learn it very well." "By the way, Roy! Would you please explain a little about this game which I think is football?" "Yes, this game is the most popular game or it's better to say the most popular sport among the people of the world." "That's right. When I was watching TV, a lot of news was said about this sport. Many of the channels showed football or said some news about it. Nowadays football is considered as the most important and popular sport. Football is a communal play in which 22 individuals play in two 45-minutes halves. Each team consists of eleven players that one of them plays as a goal keeper and the others as defense, half back or invader. In this play the players are not allowed to use their hands and should move the ball with their feet and put it in the goal. Of course they can use their heads, too. Three people take charge as a referee of the match that the most important of them is the middle referee. The middle referee runs together with the players in order to see all of the scenes and events of the match from near. If a player makes an inadmissible foul such as hitting the rival player deliberately, the referee will show him a red or yellow card that the red card means that player should leave the play ground. Besides if a player receives two yellow cards, the referee will give him a red card and fire him from the match." "It's an interesting play." "There are some other rules that you will be familiar with them later." "I couldn't play this game in your computer today, but now by your explanations I think I can do it." "Yes, it's better to play with each other." They played for about 30 minutes. Then Roy went to bring the tripod, bush and other painting instruments. They were covered with dust. Roy cleaned them and brought them to his room. His mother became surprised that Roy brought those instruments again after several years. Roy had a great talent in painting. Although he had never gone to the painting class, he drew beautiful painting. However, he had quit painting so many years ago without any reason. "John! These things are a little old, but still are safe and sound. I bought oil color and some painting papers as well. Now I think you have whatever required for painting," said Roy. "Yes, that's great," said daVinci. DaVinci, who wanted to paint again after a couple of days, started painting immediately. He was drawing an oil color painting from one part of Roy's room. He continued drawing for about half an hour. It seemed that the painting was completed, but he added some details which made the painting more real and finished the painting. From the beginning Roy sat near daVinci and looked at his painting carefully. After the painting was completed, daVinci asked Roy about the consisting materials of the colors and also the way with which they were made. "Roy! From what materials these colors are made?" asked daVinci. "From chemical materials and compounds," said Roy. "I do not understand what you mean." "The answer of your question or any other question like this is related to the chemistry science." "What is chemistry science? Can you teach me that?" "Chemistry is a science in which required things are made by the combination, or alteration of different materials and elements. These things include everything such as, clothes, colors, washing materials, papers and so on. But about teaching this science I should say that this is a complex science and most often the chemists and scientists know this science. But this doesn't mean that if someone doesn't know the chemistry, he couldn't use it. Nowadays the scientists and chemists prepare the different goods and materials by cooperation of companies and factories and supply them to the market and people can buy them with an economical cost. John! The method by which these materials are made is more complex then I can explain it for you and even I myself do not know. Forget about it, John! I want to ask you something. Can you teach me drawing?" "Yes, but it's not possible in one hour, it requires practice and time." "That's great because I'm not in hurry. John! Today I want to acquaint you with a completely new thing." "What is it?" "A thing which will revolutionize your life and will teach you so many things that you don't know." Roy turned on the computer and sat behind the computer desk and daVinci also sat next to him. "Is it complicated?" asked daVinci. "No, not at all. It's simple. You should just be careful. Well, first hold the mouse with your hand. Okay now move the pointer on the monitor and place it on the green part which is the corner of the bottom bar. Now click one time," said Roy. "By click do you mean pressing the finger on the left side of the mouse?" asked daVinci. "Yes, from now on whenever I say click, I mean pressing the left side of the mouse, and wherever I say right click, I mean pressing the right side of the mouse." "I get it. Now what should I do?" "In this blue rectangle, move the pointer of the mouse. See when you move the pointer in different parts of this rectangle, its color will change. Another point is that when you move the mouse on each of the writings in front of which is an arrow, another rectangle will be opened in front of it which is called menu." "Yes, that's right." "But the new thing which I want to teach you starts from the writing in front of which is an arrow I mean the connect option." "Now what should I do?" "From the menu in front of the connect option, select the first option, that is, ASD. This is the name of the company which offers wireless internet. Now in this new rectangle click on the connect option. Very well, it just takes some seconds in order to connect to the internet. Now we are connected." "Well, what did happen?" "A very important thing took place. Now move the pointer on the last icon which you see on the left side of the page. Now click. Of course in some computers you have to do double click to open the program. But I changed my computer's settings and you should just click one time on the icons. Each time you click on that icon this program which is called internet browser will be opened. This programmed is so easy to use. You can get information whatever that you want. I should tell you that I choose my favorite search engine as home page of my internet browser. For getting your intended information, you should just type its subject in this rectangle and then click on the search option and then another page will be opened that if you click on each of the blue writings, you will see your intended information." So Roy acquainted daVinci with internet and the method of searching in the internet. The thing which was interesting for Roy was the quick development of daVinci in learning computer. Davinci spent several hours in the internet and searching. Now he was confronted with lots of information and knowledge about his surrounding. Now he can get any information about everything in the modern world. Roy was changed a little after being acquainted with daVinci. He never liked driving before and did not want to participate in the driving license test, but now he changed his mind. He wanted to prepare himself for the driving license test from that day. Although Roy learned driving when he was 12 years old, he had never showed any interest in receiving driving license. Roy was so happy that daVinci caused some positive revolutions in his life. And this sense made him not to be upset about that event which caused daVinci to come to his time. Moreover, when he saw that daVinci himself didn't so sad of coming to the present time, he did not blame himself anymore. However, he was still thinking about finding a solution for returning daVinci to his own time .He reviewed the scenes which happened on that day in the exhibition. It seemed that a point was concealed from Roy's mind .He himself and daVinci were aware that the main factor of this event was the necklace, but none of them didn't know how those things happened. Roy knew that he had to use the necklace again in order to find a solution for the current problem. However, he was not ready to do this task. He was still shocked and could not believe that this event had really happened to him. He felt that he should wait some days later and give himself a chance to act more judiciously and his fear also reduced in order to be able to find a correct solution. The only thing which caused Roy to be relaxed was Sara. He decided to go to his favorite coffee shop with Sara. He did not still want his parents to be aware of his contacts with Sara. So he decided to behave cautiously. He called Sara and after Sara accepted his invitation, he prepared himself to go out. It was 7:30 and made an appointment with Sara on 8 o'clock. Roy decided to go with daVinci that his parents would not doubt about his behaviors. Roy was not interested in going out with his friends so much and his parents know this well. He may go to the restaurant or coffee shop with his friends just one or two times a year. He put John in the picture, too. "Hey, John! You should also come with me," said Roy. "Do you think that it's necessary? Don't you say that you want to go to a coffee shop with your fiancée?" "Yes, but my parents still do not know that Sara and I are engaged and for the current time I don't like to tell them any thing about this matter." "Why? Tell them. They should finally know." "For the time being I don't want them to know." "Okay, whatever you like." "See, John! I want to go with you that my parents can not make head of my tasks. Do you get it?" "Yes I do." "So if my parents ask you where you are going to, you should say that we are going out to continue our research project and also to meet other members of our research team." "Okay, I get it." "It's better to go and change your clothes and prepare yourself for going out. It's near 8 o'clock." "By the way, Roy! Are we going by your father's car?" "No, forget about it. We lent his car for two successive nights. I can not even think about it. At least for the time begin." "Can't you satisfy your father in any way?" "It's not related to his satisfaction. I feel shame to lend his car every night. Moreover, do you think about the troubles we may face if we lend Dad's car? None of us have a driving license and you yourself even don't have an identification card so it's better to forget lending Dad's car. We will go by taxi." "What is a taxi?" "Don't be confused, man! A taxi is the same as the car, but its only difference is that it's not a private automobile. The taxi driver takes the people of the city in exchange for money." "It's too strange. Do you mean that a driver takes all of the people of the city by one car?" "No, there are a lot of taxies and drivers in each city. Hurry up, man! Don't hesitate. Go and change your clothes." They became ready after some minutes and every thing happened as Roy had programmed and his parents also accepted that matter as Roy had expected. They arrived there five minutes earlier than 8 o'clock. "Sara will come soon. John! Sit at one of the tables and wait until our conversation finishes and if we go out of the coffee shop, you follow us, too and wait until I say goodbye to Sara, and then we will come back home with each other. By the way, if the waiter asks you what do you want, say coffee glass and if he wants money, point to me and say that man will pay it. Do you get it?" "Yes, I do." "So go and sit there." It was still one minute to eight when Sara came. "Hi" "Hi, Roy! How are you?" "Fine, sit down." Then the waiter came and after they selected their favorite drink, they continued their talks. Roy said while he didn't know what to say, "I' m so pleased that you accept my invitation. To tell you the truth, from the time I have seen you my feelings toward life are changed. You are the only girl who caused me to look at the life differently." "Can you explain more clearly?" "Well, before I met you I did not feel love toward any girl. But you....just you could change me." "I have these feeling, too, but when I understand that you loved me, my love toward you intensified. When I saw you for the first time, I had good feeling toward you. I felt that I love you, but I doubt it. But when I understood that you love me, too, my feeling changed to real and now I completely feel that

I love you." "That day when I saw you in font of your house, I couldn't forget you even for a moment. I saw you wherever I went and whatever I did. I couldn't sleep at nights. I just thought about you." "Very well, Roy! I know that you love me, but I like to be acquainted with you and your life more and you yourself know me better." "If you want to know me better, it's better to ask your brother about me because he is one of my close and intimate friends." "Of course I asked David about you, but I like to know you better." "Okay, you can ask me whatever you like." "Very well, but I hope you didn't be offended." "No, not at all. You're right." "Roy! Love is the most important factor in the marriage, but there are other things which affect the stability and quality of life." "Yes, of course." "Is money more important for you or love?" "It's obvious. Love." "If we marry in the future, how important is having children for you?" "To tell you the truth, I love having children, but if it isn't possible, it won't be important for me. And I still make all of my efforts to improve our life." "What are your hobbies?" "Computer games are one of the most important of my hobbies, but I also like listening to the music or watching concerts and video clips of my favorite singers. By the way, what are your hobbies?" "My hobbies are very different from yours. The most important one is horseback riding. I like horseback riding and, generally, the horses. And most often I go to the horse riding club. But I really like to have a stable at home and keep my horse there. After horse riding I like tennis. By the way, Roy! Tell me about your friends. How many friends do you have?" "I have a lot of friends, but I just have a close relationship with two or there of them. Generally I spend most of my time at home and I don't spend my time with my friend." "What are you going to do after graduation? I mean do you want to work or continue your studying?" "Well, I don't know exactly, but I think after receiving my B.A, I will work." "If you want to work in the future, which of them will be more important for you? Your job or your family?" "Well, your answer is totally obvious, my family and personal life are more important than working." "Roy! It's better to go." And Roy paid the money of his drink and Sara's and also davinci's. Then they went out of the coffee shop. As they were walking slowly, they talked with each other. "Roy! I want to ask you a very important question. Its answer is very important for me. But before asking, I should tell you that I just want to know you better by this question and I don't intend to make you worried." "I told you that you can ask whatever you like." "If you miss me for any reason or for example, I break off my relations with you, will you think about any other girl?" Roy, who became a bit surprised and confused by this question, said, "of course not, because I just love you. If I wanted to marry another girl, I would do it before. But I only love you." "Roy! Nice to meet you. I should go right now." "Thanks for your coming bye." "Bye." After Sara went farther from Roy, he went toward daVinci who stood near him. "Well, John! Let's go." "You seem a little worried. You are not so happy to see your fiancée." "I'm so pleased, but her words are a little queer." "Roy! Before we return home, can I ask you something?" "Yes, say it." "Would you take me to a cinema?" "How do you learn the word cinema?" "From TV." "I don't think that we have enough time to go to the cinema." "You mean it's not possible to go the cinema tonight." Roy said more seriously, "No." "But you told your parents that you wanted to continue a research project with me while this is not true. Moreover what will happen if you take me to a cinema?" "John! You should not be offended." "Don't say anything. You don't want to go to the cinema with me." "Roy said softly, "okay, but I myself should choose the movie." "It doesn't matter." "There is a cinema over there. We will go there right now. By the way, John! Which kind of film do you like?" "I don't know exactly because it's the first time that I want to go to the cinema, but I think a comedy one is better. When I was watching TV, the most attractive programmers for me were comedy ones." "Now I know which film I should choose." They walked until they arrived at a cinema. Then they bought two tickets and entered the cinema daVinci was so excited that he just gazed at the display scene. Roy stood up and went to buy some refreshments. He bought some pop corn and chips and came back soon and sat beside daVinci. "Where did you go?" "I went to buy some pop corn and chips. While you are watching the film, eat these things." "What is pop corn and chips?" When the person, who was sitting next to daVinci, heard that, turned his head toward them and looked at them surprisingly. Roy whispered in daVinci's ear, "When thin and sliced potatoes are fried in the oil, a delicious thing will be made which is called chips. And if kernels are heated, they will puff up and another delicious thing will be made which is called pop corn." "Now do you get it?" "Yes, I do." Roy said as before, "Another time you want to ask me something, try to ask in a way that the others won't think you are foolish." "Okay." Roy said with his usual sound and tone, "John! I hope you weren't offended by my words." "No, I don't mind." "So while you are watching the film, eat pop corn and chips" "Okay, I will eat." Soon after the film was started, the refreshments which Roy had bought finished. DaVinci liked them so much. "Roy! Can you buy a bit more of these refreshments?" "Yes, I'll go and buy some right now." "I like chips more." Roy went and bought some chips and pop corn, but this time he also bought two coca cola. This time before daVinci had started asking Roy, he whispered in his ear, "John! These two things which are in my hand are coca cola. A kind of sweet drink that has bubbles in it and can help the digestion of the food." "Thanks for telling me before I start asking you." "I hope you weren't offended. I thought with myself that it's better to tell you before you ask." Then Roy lowered his voice again that just daVinci could hear him and said, "By the way pull the metal grip toward you to open it and then start drinking it." "I get it." It was 10:30 and the film was finished. They were so excited by watching that movie that they forgot it was 10:30 at night and they had to come back home. Roy was also so surprised that he enjoyed so much. When they went out of the cinema, they had just found themselves. Although that film was so funny, it couldn't attract Roy's attention. Roy seemed a little worried. Sara's words were slightly strange. Sara had asked Roy suspicious questions several times which made him worried. However, Roy didn't dodge to answer her questions and he answered all of her questions honestly. Sara's tone of speaking was so different from the previous time and Roy had understood this matter well. This time boldness and outspokenness were exited in Sara's words instead of intimacy and love. However, Roy thought that Sara had a right to know more about her future mate. It was 11:00 when Roy and daVinci arrived home. Roy was a little afraid that during recent days he had spent most of his time with daVinci. However, he was happy because he was experiencing a new period in his life which was full of bravery and independence in making decisions and risking. Of course for him risking meant the possibility of getting into troubles, but he willingly welcomed the new facts of life. Until that time Roy never went out with his friends up to that late at night. But from when daVinci entered his life, each day he had experienced new things. This new season of life was considered as a common fact for his age group, but it was considered to be totally new for Roy who was dependent to his family. Fortunately

Roy's parents had also accepted his behavioral changes. When Roy got home, he was frightened from his parents' reaction, but after several minutes he understood that they won't behave sharply. Roy felt tired and after changing his clothes, he went to his bed. His body was at home and on the bed, but his soul was still in that coffee shop with Sara, as if his soul was remained at that time. His mind couldn't understand Sara's words well. Although Roy felt that the only thing which was weighing on his mind was Sara, there was still another important matter and that was financial independence. Successive spending money and paying the cost of amusements which Roy had caused for Roy made him to feel weakness financially. Although Roy's family was rich and wealthy and Roy was the only son, he had been confronted with a completely different concept. He knew that if he asked his parents to give him more money, they would do it, but the thing which was important for him was not to be dependent to his parents financially. He had spent a lot of money during those days. He didn't want his parents to think that he was a prodigal boy. He was thinking about this matter that he himself earn money. Due to his skills, finding a good job was not so difficult for him. But he sought a job that he could earn so much money without spending a lot of time and preferably at home. Although his university field of study didn't related to the computer, he had many skills in the computer affairs. Roy felt that his life was moving gradually in a different way than before. Although he was satisfied with the new changes and revolutions of his life, he was afraid a little which was created due to lack of self confidence. The next day Kathy's behavior with Roy was a little different and strange. She was talking in a way as if she had expected a special event occurring in Roy's life. Roy couldn't understand Kathy's words. He didn't pay too much attention to her words and tried to forget them and thought about more important things. Roy had used to concentrate on lessons in the class and didn't allow himself to think about other things. And this caused him to be tired of learning lessons and concentrating on them in the class. The recent happenings and also the new kind of life which he had experienced during those days caused him to have bad feelings toward his previous life which was considered to be ideal for him. Roy was in class physically, but mentally he wasn't there and he didn't pay any attention to the class and lessons. Sitting in the place which he didn't like and excessive activity made Roy tired. Roy had much interest in studying and generally in acquiring knowledge and this interest existed in him from the childhood. Roy was the best student in the high school. He always made his effort to get the best scores and learn more than the others. And this was also true about him at the university. Roy was one of the best and known students of the university. But it seemed that he didn't have enough energy for this type of life full of mental and scientific activities. Although he had excessive interest in acquiring knowledge and success in his field of study, he felt that he had needed rest a lot that he didn't go to the university for several months in order to reduce his tiredness. But he felt that he wasn't in a situation to do this task. He didn't like Sara and his parents think he was incapable. And if he was unsuccessful in his education, they would certainly think like this about him and may even blame him. And Roy didn't want to confront with this situation. He came to this conclusion that he should make all of his efforts to be successful in his education. After his class finished, Roy understood that his efforts were useless and his mind was so disrupted that he couldn't concentrate on the lessons. The event at the exhibition, entering daVinci to his life, returning daVinci to his own time, loving Sara and being afraid to miss her, doubting about his kind of life,... are thoughts which made Roy worried that he couldn't think about anything else. However, his main worry was not about learning his university lessons because he could easily learn them at home by his talent. His main worry was about daVinci. He thought it was his fault that caused daVinci to come to the present time, while he even didn't know how he could return him to his time and solve the current problem. That day when his classes finished, he borrowed Kathy's notes to scan them and save them in his computer. Kathy was a diligent student and she took notes from every important points of class and for this reason Roy thought that her notes could help him in learning. "Would you please lend me your notes? I will return them tomorrow," said Roy. "Yes, I will give it to you. Roy! It seems that you are a little worried. Today you didn't pay any attention to the lessons. Is there anything wrong with you?" said Kathy. "No, I just feel tired." "If there is anything wrong with you, you can count on me." "No, everything is all right." "Anyhow, I hope so. I just asked because I am worried about you." "Thanks, Kathy! I am just tired. I think this is because of my cold." Then Roy took the notes from Kathy and said goodbye to her and went. As usual Davis was waiting for him in front of the entrance door of the university in order to come back home with each other. "Hi," said Roy. "Hi," said David. "Today I want to go to the driving office to participate in the driving license test." "Really? How did you change your mind? You said that you didn't like driving." "Well sometimes you say something, but later you will change your mind." "Don't you want to get a driving license due to your new friend whose name is John?" "Maybe, but I should do this some day." "Yes, you're right." "If you want, you can come back home alone." "No, we will go with each other." They went by metro as the usual. Roy was not worried about the driving license test because he could drive well and he had to learn driving symbols and regulations. After registration, he bought the guidance book of driving laws and regulations from there. Then they went to the metro station and got on the train in order to come back home. On the way to come back home Roy felt a special self confidence and bravery. He was sure that he would be accepted in the driving license test. Now he understood that life was not just sitting at home to study or plays a computer game. His happiness became more when he remembered that his father had promised to buy a car for him if he could get his driving license. When he arrived home, he said this matter to his parents and they also became happy. "I'm so happy that you finally decide to get your driving license after several years," said Kathryn. "You behave in a way that I think you will never get your driving license," said Steven. "Don't be too happy since I just register in the test and I have not got the driving license yet," said Roy. "Roy! I am sure that you will be accepted. Your driving is very good." said Steven. "By the way, Dad! Don't you remember something by getting a driving license?" asked Roy. "Like what?" asked Steven. "That you had promised me something or..." "Oh, now I get it. So you remember what I promised you several years ago." "Well, I myself forget it. I just remember it by accident." "If you get your driving license, be sure that I will do it." "Oh, Dad! I am kidding." "But I was serious, whenever you get a driving license, I will buy you a car." "It's better to talk about it later." "Okay" when Roy was going to his room, Kathryn said to him while she hold a big plastic sack, "By the way, whose clothes are these?" Roy took a look at that sack. He saw the old clothes of daVinci. He was shocked and didn't know what to say. After a hesitation, he said, "I took these clothes from the theatre group of our university. I will play a role in the theatre group of the university. For this reason I borrowed these clothes from them to practice me role." "Very good, you are active in art as well as scientific and research affairs," said Kathryn. "Yes, one of my friends suggested me to play this role and I accepted." "It's very well. Art works make your mind be more active. Give these clothes. You're lucky that I didn't throw them out." Then Roy took daVinci's clothes from Kathryn and went to his room and put them under his bed. "Hi," said daVinci. "Hi, you are lucky that my mother didn't throw your real clothes out. But don't worry; I put them under my bed. You will need them when you want to come back to your time," said Roy. "Yes, you're right," said daVinci. "What are those papers?" asked Roy. "It was strange for me, too. I was working with that thing which you taught me yesterday, the one by which you said we can get information." "Do you mean internet?" "Yes, I was working with the internet that suddenly when I click on a small square painting like that box, a colorful paper came out of that box." "Now I get what you mean. You click on the print icon. And that box is called printer. Give me those papers that I can see them, too." "This printer is a very strange machine. How it can paint so rapidly?" "Wow, how beautiful pictures you printed!" "I found them in the internet." "That's great, John! You are really talented. It's just a few days that you are acquainted with the computer, but you can search pictures in the internet." "Well, everything was simple as you said before, but I can't still understand how those pictures come out of that box." "Don't confuse yourself. It's just a kind of machine. It's not important to know how it works sine it's a little hard to explain. It's enough that you can work with it. It's better to turn off the computer because I want to watch TV with its monitor." "Roy! You have taught me so many things about computer, but you have not taught me how to turn it off." "Okay, I'll teach you right now. See you should click on this corner on the left side on which 'start' is written. Afterwards a menu will be opened and you should click on this square in the middle of which is a red circle. Then a rectangle will be opened in the middle of the page and its surrounding environment will change to white and black and now for turning the computer off you should click on the central circle which is also red and then after some seconds the computer will turn off. Do you get it?" "Yes, to some extent." Then Roy started watching TV. He used to watch daily news on his favorite channel. A news was also broadcasted about the exhibition and disappearing some of the paintings. Several days had passed from the day that a number of paintings of the exhibition, which held in the New York museum, had lost. But it was still considered as one of the most important news. Disappearing of the paintings was still mysterious for police.

But anyhow a number of the most important and beautiful paintings of daVinci were disappeared. Roy, who seemed worried after hearing that news, turned off TV. It was obvious from his face that he was thinking about an important issue. "By the way what's wrong with the exhibition and robbed paintings? By daVinci do they mean me? How did we appear in that exhibition on that day?" "For your first question I should say yes, they mean you. Your paintings are considered as the most expensive and unique paintings all around the world and you yourself is a famous person in our time and most of the people around the world know you. If you think well, you see why those people laughed at you on the first day you came to our time. Do you remember?" "Yes, that day when I came to your time. Do you want to say that they thought I was crazy?" "Yes, since you belong to several centuries ago, they were sure that you were crazy. I'm sorry to say that, I didn't want to ridicule you. I just want you to understand though you don't live in our time, most of the people know you." "I know what you mean." "But about your second question I should say that wasn't my fault and one of my friends gave me the ticket of your paintings exhibition and we made an appointment to meet each other there. But I arrived there a little early. I was watching the paintings. But when I gazed at one of them, that event took place. I just carried a necklace which my grandfather gifted me. Of course my grandfather had told me that it wasn't a usual necklace, but I didn't consider them serious. I think he himself thinks it is a usual necklace. He told me that he had bought that necklace from an African native. Grandpa said that native man told him it wasn't a usual necklace and it was magical. To tell you the truth it was hard for me to believe it is magical and even it was ridiculous for me. But after that event I am sure that everything is related to that necklace."

Then Roy held the necklace in his hand and looked at it. But he didn't dare to put it around his neck again. "Can you explain more precisely? How far you were from the painting when you were at the exhibition? Can you tell me more details about that day?" asked daVinci. "Well, I was in the half meter from the painting, that is, the distance between me and the painting was about one foot and the necklace was also around my neck." "Can you tell me how did you hang it around your neck?" "I put it in a way that its green side was forward and the blue side was backward. DaVinci took the necklace from Roy and looked at it and said, "It's too strange. The shape of the both side is exactly like an eye, a green eye and a blue eye." "Yes, it's strange. Eye, picture, look all of them are related to each other." "On that day you wore this necklace was it on your shirt or under it?" "It was under my shirt." "Can you explain one more time on that moment you entered my room what was exactly happened?" "I was looking at one of the paintings of the exhibition just for 2 or perhaps 3 seconds that I felt I weren't at the exhibition space and I quickly understood that place wasn't the exhibition since its light was more than your room." "Did you gaze only at that painting or you gazed at the other paintings, too?" "I just gazed at that painting since it was the first one at which I wanted to look." "Well, so up to now we can conclude that because you put on that necklace and gazed at that painting, you came to my time who is the painter of that painting. And according to your words we should say that since its green side was forward, it caused you to come to my time. And it's interesting that when I just finished that painting, you were behind me." "You mean that the necklace will bring the person, who looks at the painting, to the time when it was drawn. Well up to now we get something about the necklace. But now we should think about how we came from your room to my time that is the year 2006." "You were standing near me and talking to me and our distance was short. At least at the last moment we were in my room our distance was too short." "Yes, I think it was less than one meter." "I exactly remember that a few seconds before we went to your time you brought out the necklace from your shirt and then we were at the exhibition." "Yeah, now I remember. At that moment I brought out the necklace from my shirt and showed you its blue side and after some seconds we weren't there and were transferred to the exhibition." "So we can conclude that since you held the blue side of the necklace toward me and in fact you changed the side of the necklace both of us came to your time. It means that when you reversed the necklace, its function was also reversed." "But there is still a vague thing. Why did you come together with me to my time?" "Were there any other people around you when you were at the exhibition?"

"At that time the exhibition was not crowded and there were just five or six persons there, but they were far from me." "But when I came to your time, I stood near you and for this reason I came together with you." "So it was because of our short distance that we came with each other to this time. But one thing is still strange for me." "What?" "Why some of the paintings have lost at the exhibition? They weren't stolen or lost. In fact they were not existed anymore." "What do you mean? Are they vanished?" "Yes, but when you come back to your time, they will return to their places again." "If I don't come back to my time or I can not do that, what will happen then?" "Well in this case, those paintings will never return and they will vanish forever." "You want to say that those paintings are vanished since they belong to the time after I come to your time." "Yes, that's right." "Now we know a lot about the necklace and its function and also the event took place and we can say that we find the solution of our problem." "Yes, now we know how to solve this problem. But first we should test our hypothesis on the necklace to see how we can return you to your time." Roy decided to put on the necklace again but as soon as he wanted to pick up his hands and hang the necklace around his neck, he changed his mind and decided to wait a little more. "John! Although I almost know how this necklace works, it's better to act more logically. In your opinion what should we do now?" "Don't you have a painting or picture which is suitable for testing the necklace?" "Wait a minute to bring my photo albums in order to choose one." Then Roy pulled out one of his drawers and brought out his last photo album. "In my opinion it's better to choose a picture in which no one exists," said Roy. "I think those pictures which I got from internet are better," said daVinci. "It sounds like a good idea." Then Roy started looking at the pictures which daVinci got from internet. He selected the photo which was taken from the liberty statue. "John! I think this is the most suitable photo." "Are you ready to test the necklace?" "Yes, I will try it up to several minutes later." "I don't want you to be in trouble for the sake of me." "All of these troubles are due to my mistake. I disrupted your life." "No, Roy! This is not your fault. Don't blame yourself. You didn't put on the necklace on purpose." "But I should do this task even if it is dangerous. I will never forgive myself if I can not return you to your own time." This event I mean coming to your time is not so bad for me and in my opinion it's interesting. Even if I can not come back to my time, you should not blame yourself." "To tell you the truth it is good for me, too, but I hope you are not offended by me." "So put away the necklace for now. Don't do it for the sake of me." "John! I make my decision and according to our previous experience I don't think it's dangerous." "Okay, try it." Then Roy put on the necklace. Roy was afraid that testing the necklace leads to new problems. But he made his decision to test the necklace. He wanted to compensate for his mistake and returned daVinci to his own time. He considered himself responsible for the lost paintings. "Roy! Remember that the green side brings you inside the picture and the blue side can return you. Do you get it?" "Yes, I do. You go farther in order not to come with me." "No, it's better to be with each other." "But I don't want to get you in trouble again." "No, what trouble? I won't leave you alone." "Okay, are you ready?" "Yes, now you can look at the picture." Then Roy gazed at the picture. Soon after 3 seconds both of them felt that they were standing in front of the Liberty Statue and exactly behind a young photographer. "Hey, John! We are in front of the Liberty Statue. And that photographer is the one who took that picture." "Yes, that's right." That photographer looked at them surprisingly and went. "Well, now we should do the second part of our work.

That is returning to that place that we were." "Reverse the necklace, I mean put the blue side forward." Roy did this task and they returned to Roy's room. Roy removed the necklace quickly. He was so happy. Both of them felt that their problem was solved completely. "Everything was well-done," said Roy. "Yes, do your mind at ease in returning me to my time?" "Yeah, for returning you we should just go to the exhibition and stand in front of that painting which I gazed at and everything will be finished." As soon as Roy uttered the word exhibition he felt worried. He didn't pay attention to this feeling for some seconds, but soon after this thought came to his mind that maybe the exhibition was closed. "John! Go and change your clothes right now. We have to go." "What's matter, Roy? Where should we go?" "We should go to the exhibition." "Now?" "Yes, right now. It may become late even now." Roy quickly brought out his cell phone from the pocket of his trousers and called the museum and talked to the authority of the exhibition. The person, whom Roy talked to, said that day was the last day of the exhibition and gave him a telephone number to make a reservation. Roy called that number, but the man who was in charge of selling the tickets said that all of the tickets were sold from a few days ago. Roy asked him several times what he could do to buy a ticket, but he just said he was sorry. Roy was so worried and anxious. He was aware that if he couldn't go to the exhibition with daVinci, how hard it would be to return him to his time. Roy didn't even know what was the name of that painting or to which country it would be brought after the exhibition was closed. He couldn't do anything except knowing whose painting was that or where the owner of that painting lived. "John! You don't need to change your clothes," said Roy. "What's the matter? Can't you reserve a ticket?" "No, we are unlucky. All of the tickets were sold from several days ago. Now the only way of accessing to the painting is finding its owner." "Don't you say that it is at the exhibition?" "Yes, it is at the exhibition, but just up to the end of today." "What does it mean? Do you mean it's not at the exhibition tomorrow?" "No, it's not there because today is the last day of the exhibition. And this means that we lost the painting which we need for returning you to your time." "It's not important. It's enough that we learn the way of returning." "That's right, but our task becomes so hard because it's not so easy to achieve that painting. Even for renting or watching this painting for some minutes we have to pay so much money, provided its owner or the museum authorities accept that. We even don't know whose painting it is. If the painting belongs to a museum of another country or this country, it will be easier. But if the painting belongs to a person, it's unlikely that he will permit us to have the accessibility to the painting." "Don't worry, Roy! We will finally find a solution." "I'm not worried. I'm just afraid of this matter that we can not have accessibility to that painting anymore. I even don't know the name of that painting." "By the way, Roy! Why don't you use that thing by which you said we can get any information? I mean internet." "Yeah, you're right. I forget that we can use the internet." They first found among the works of daVinci the name of that painting and also its owner. The painting had belonged to a collector, but more information about him was not written on that page. They just could find the name and nationality of that collector. After some minutes they could find the email address and also the personal web site of the owner of that painting by other web sites. After some searching through the pages of the web site, they could find his telephone number and address. He lived in New York and this caused them to be less worried. "Now we have his name, address, telephone number and email address. I'm just afraid he won't be satisfied that we see the painting from near. Even if he let us see the painting, it's unlikely that he will leave us alone with the painting," said Roy. "Yes. You're right," said daVinci. "We should wait some more days and act more logically." "Yeah, it's better to forget about it now." Then Roy started studying the driving laws and regulations book. Afterwards Kathryn came to his room and told them to go for dinner. After having dinner, Roy thought again to find a way to earn money at home. He paid several thousands dollars during the past days. Although he knew that his father would give him money as much as he wanted, his pride prevented him to ask his father to give him money. He was sure that by his skills he could find a job by which he could earn 10 to 15 thousands dollars during one or two weeks. The best option for Roy to work at home was computer programming and creating three dimensional graphics by computer. He remembered the address of a web site which worked in the field of creating three dimensional graphics. Roy went to that web site and sent an email to their email address. They replied Roy's email very quickly and it was written in that email that Roy should sign the contract note which was sent together with the email and then send it again to the email address of that company. Roy had bought the last version of Maya software and installed it in his computer. Roy started his work from that night. He felt a special self confidence. This was the first time that Roy used his abilities in earning money. His computer was powerful and he didn't have any problem in rendering the scenes. He could design the main characters of animation in the early hours of his work, but it still needed more details. It was 11:45 and he was still working. He was sure that if the work continued well, he could deliver it earlier. "Roy! What are you doing?" asked daVinci. "I'm creating a three dimensional animation. This is a three- minute advertisement," said Roy. "What is the use of this advertising animation?" "After I make this animation and deliver it to the company with which I have made a contract, they will record sound on it and then it will broadcast on television as an advertisement." "So what's the use of it for you?" "If I can deliver it to them on time according to the contract, they should give me 10 thousand dollars." "How long dose it need to be finished?" "About two weeks. During this week I need the computer so much and in this case you can use laptop to play or connect to the internet." "Okay." Roy saved his work on the mp3 player in order to be able to continue his work in metro or any other places. Then he turned off the computer. DaVinci went to his room and both of them slept. Next day in the university Roy experienced a completely different day with previous days. Unlike several past days that he didn't have concentration on his lessons; on that day he learnt his lessons with complete concentration, motivation and self-confidence. He didn't feel tired in the class. After his first class finished, in the break he talked to Kathy. She talked more suspiciously this time. She spoke in away that she didn't expect Roy to become fine soon. But Roy doubted more when Kathy talked about his fiancée unwillingly. But she tried to pretend that his personal life wasn't important for her, while in fact that wasn't true. "Roy! You are such a very strange person. One day you seem so tired and upset that you can not do your daily tasks and the other day you are so energetic that it seems you can move a mountain," said Kathy. "I told you that I just caught a cold and for this reason I didn't feel good," said Roy. "Well sometimes I myself feel tired, but yesterday you were so upset that I thought maybe your fiancée left you." "Do you mean Sara, my fiancée? We have a very good relationship with each other." "Was there anything wrong between you and Sara yesterday?" "No. Yesterday nothing had happened between us." "I hope you are not offended by my words." "No, I don't." "By the way you didn't say why you are so energetic today." "Because everything is all right as I expected." "Anyhow I'm so happy to see you are glad and energetic." The break finished and they went to class. On the way to come back home, Roy continued working on his project instead of playing computer games in the metro. When he got home, he continued working after eating lunch, unlike everyday that he rested for several hours or slept. He worked on creating animation and rendering the new frames for about 3 hours and then he studied his lessons. It was 500 in the afternoon. Although he had so much motivation for working, he decided to rest for a while. He was lying on his bed that his cell phone rang. He didn't want to answer that call, but it seemed that the one who called him didn't want to cut off the phone. He stood up from the bed and picked up his cell phone. Sara's number was displayed on the monitor. As soon as he understood it was Sara, he answered the phone. "Hello, is this you, Sara?" "Yes, I am." "I'm sorry to answer late." "It doesn't matter." "How are you?" "I'm fine. Well I'm calling you to tell you an important thing." "What's that?" "It's very difficult for me to say that, but you should know the fact." "What fact?" "How can I say...I...I..." "You what? What do you want to say?" "I don't want to be engaged with you anymore." "But, why?" "I can not say anything more." "How do you decide suddenly not to be engaged with me anymore?" "I have thought about this a lot and I don't want to have any relationship with you." "But..." And then Sara cut off the phone. Roy was shocked. He couldn't believe it. He was so anxious and shocked that his face became red. He was sitting on the sofa and couldn't say anything. "What's wrong with you, Roy?" asked daVinci. But Roy was still silent. He felt that without Sara he couldn't even breathe. He was silent for some minutes and didn't say anything to daVinci. Then he said, "Sara is going to leave me." "Are you talking about your fiancée?" "Yes." "I'm sorry." "She doesn't want to see me anymore and she told me that I should confront with reality." "But don't you say that you love each other, so how did she suddenly make such a decision?" "I don't know. She didn't tell me the reason." "Roy! Grieving is of no use. You should behave more logically and talk to her and see why she made such a decision." "But just a few days ago she said that she loved me. I love her so much. I feel that I can not live without her." "You should see her as soon as possible. It's still possible to change her mind." "I have a very bad feeling. I feel even I can not move." "It's okay. Everything will be all right. It's because you are shocked. You will be better up to some minutes later." "But I can not live without her." "See, Roy! I know well that you love her, but it seems that a factor made her leave you and do not have any relationship with you." "In your opinion what should I do now?" "You should find that factor. That can be everything, for example another man or boy, Sara's family, her future or anything else. I know that it's hard for you to accept it, but you should find that factor before it becomes late. Maybe you can solve the problem. But if you just love her or she just pretended to love you in the past, unfortunately I should say that you have to forget her." "But she said several times that she loved me." "Maybe she was just pretending and another thing caused her to continue her relationship with you." "I can not understand. I don't know what I should do." "Call her right now." Roy picked up her cell phone and dialed Sara's number, but she didn't answer. "She doesn't answer on purpose. She knows my number." "It doesn't matter. Call again." And Roy dialed her again, but she didn't answer. It seemed that she didn't want to talk to him anymore. This idea came to his mind that if his number did not display on her phone, she would not understand that was Roy and would answer. He turned on his computer and after connecting to the internet; he quickly entered voip system and dialed Sara's number. This time she answered the phone. "Hello," said Sara. "Hello, Sara! I know you don't want to talk to me, but please don't cut off the phone for some minutes. Why do change suddenly? Why don't you tell me the reason?" "I know that it's hard for you to accept it, but I don't want to have any relationship with you. Maybe you love me, but I don't love you. So don't call me." "But can you just tell me its reason? Do you love another man?" "I don't want to tell you the reason of my tasks, but I should say that I don't intend to marry and I also don't love another boy. But this is not related to you." "But why?" "I don't want to talk to you anymore. Maybe I'll tell you the reason of my decisions in the future, but now I can not say anything." "Did I do something wrong?"

"Don't call me." "But…" "Bye." And then she cut off the phone. Roy tried to do his works in order to forget Sara as daVinci suggested him. He continued working for several hours without resting. Afterwards Roy felt that his anxiety was reduced to some extent and working and also not thinking about Sara caused him to forget Sara. After saving his work on the hard of the computer and his mp3player, he decided to think about calling the owner of the painting. DaVinci was engaged in playing with laptop. "What do you think, John if we now call Mr. James Arthur?" said Roy. DaVinci turned off the laptop and went toward Roy and sat next to him. "It sounds like a good idea, but what should we say to him?" said daVinci. "I don't know exactly." "Don't you say that he is a very important and big shot man?" "Yes, exactly." "Communicating with such a person is very hard. We should talk to him in a way that he won't think we are going to steal the painting."

"That's right, but I hope we can contact him."
"Don't you say that now we have the telephone number, email address and home address of the owner of the painting, I mean this Mr. James Arthur?" "Yes, I said. But these kind people usually receive hundreds of emails and calls in a day that most of them do not reply them. Of course I think the best way is to send an email since these people answer the calls rarely." "We should find a way to attract his attention to ourselves." "Yes, but what can attract Mr. Arthur?" "He is an art works collector. The first thing which can attract him is a famous or expensive painting." "Yes, but we don't have any famous painting." "So we should find another way." "That's great, John. You're completely right. When we don't have any painting, the only thing which can attract him is buying that painting." "Yes, we can tell him that we want to buy that painting and he will let us see the painting from near." "But we should be very careful. We should send him an

email and tell him that we want to buy the painting. If we are lucky and he wants to sell the painting, we can be hopeful that he will let us see the painting." Roy wrote a text in which Mr. Arthur was asked whether he wanted to sell the painting. "Well, we should wait until he himself or his secretary answers our email," said Roy. "Roy! I want you to do something for me that I know it's very difficult for you, but I beg you to help me to do it," said daVinci. "What do you want to do?" "I want to go to Italy and see Florence in this present century. I miss my land and my city." "Okay no problem. We will do it right now." "But how? It's too far from here and we should go by airplane. Moreover don't you say that traveling by plane needs an identification card?" "Yes, I said, but we don't want to go by plane." "So how do you want to take me there?" Roy sat behind the computer desk again and said, "This is a web site by which you can see every part of the world. The pictures which this site shows you are taken from the sky. See these are the photos which were taken from Florence city a few seconds ago. Now we can search the pictures of various parts of the city and then watch them." "Thanks a lot, Roy! This is like that I really travel to Italy. I'm so happy to see these pictures." "Wait there is another thing. Now we can see the scenes of Florence city by a number of online web cams." Roy could show daVinci the images of Florence city by the help of live images of some online web cams and made him happy and satisfied. It was eight o'clock at night that Roy's mother entered his room and said that the dinner was ready. After eating dinner, they sat behind the computer desk again. This time they wanted to check Roy's email. Mr. Arthur had not answered his email yet. Then daVinci started painting and Roy went out of the room and went to his parents. "Dad! Would you please lend me your car? I want to practice driving," said Roy.

"Provided that you don't drive fast and be careful," said Steven. "Don't worry, Dad! John will come with me. He has a driving license." "Okay, the switch is in my pocket." Then Roy took the switch and went to his room. "John! Go and change your clothes. We want to go out," said Roy. "Where we wanna go?" "Don't you like car driving?" "Yes, but don't you say that if we drive without a driving license, the police will seize us?" "Yes, I said, but I want to practice driving." "Okay, let's go." Then they brought out the car outside and started driving on the street. Then they returned home. Soon after they arrived home, Roy turned on his computer and checked his email. After opening his box, the first thing which attracted Roy and also made him happy was the email which Mr. Arthur sent for him. Roy opened that email. Mr. Arthur himself wrote that letter and he said that the painting was sold and he was not the owner of the painting anymore. When Roy understood this matter, he became slightly upset and worried. He was aware that in this case returning daVinci to his time would be more difficult. But the thing which was not clear for Roy was that to whom that painting was sold. Mr. Arthur didn't say the name of the person to whom that painting was sold and Roy was afraid that Mr. Arthur may conceal his name. "Did you check your email?" asked daVinci. "Yes, Mr. Arthur answered our email," said Roy. DaVinci said happily, "Really? Did he answer our email?" "Don't be happy, John! Because he sold the painting." "What? He sold the painting!" "Yes, he said in the email that he sold the painting several days before the exhibition was held and it was due to submit the painting to the person who had bought it after the exhibition finished." "Did he write the name, address, or email address of the current owner of the painting in his letter?" "No, he didn't say anything about the name of the purchaser of the painting. We should send an email for Mr. Arthur right now and tell him that we want to buy that painting and we need the name and address of the current owner of the painting." "If he doesn't give us the name and address of its owner, what should we do then?" "I don't know. In this case our work has become more difficult let alone he doesn't want to tell us the name of the owner of the painting. But I don't think so; there is no reason that he will refuse to give us his name. It makes no difference that we buy the painting from him or another person." "But if the current owner of the painting had asked him not to tell the others that he sold him the painting, he won't tell us his name." "Anyhow, a few minutes ago I sent him an email to give us his name, and address. Don't worry, John!" Roy worked on his project a little more and daVinci played computer game with laptop and after half an hour both of them went to sleep. Although some hours had passed from the time when Roy went to his bed, he couldn't sleep. Separating from Sara was an event which was so difficult for Roy. Although he was completely understood that Sara didn't value his love, he couldn't forget her. His main grief was this matter that Sara didn't tell him why she would give him the elbow. It was 3:00 in the morning and Roy was still awake. He tried so much to sleep, but he couldn't. He didn't want to express his grief, but finally he started crying and tears were dropping from his eyes unwillingly. It was 3:30 that he slept. Although he slept late last night, he woke up early in the morning. He didn't have any appetite for breakfast and he just drank a coup of coffee and then he changed his clothes and put his books in his bag and went out to go to the university. As usual he waited for David to go with each other to the metro station. He was worried that the break-up in his relationship with Sara may cause David to finish his friendship with him. Some minutes had passed from the moment he was waiting that finally David came. "Hi," said Roy. "Hi," said David.

Unlike everyday they were silent until they arrived at the station. It seemed that both of them were afraid of the reaction of each other. None them knew what to say. Roy was too upset and it was obvious from his face. But the meaningful silence of David showed Roy that he was aware of that matter. They were near the station that David decided to end that silence. "Roy! I know that you are upset that Sara disrupted her relationship with you, but you should know that this matter is just related to you and Sara and I don't like it also affects our relationship," said David. "David! To tell you the truth I don't like it, too. This morning when you came later than every day, I think you are not on speaking terms with me. But when you came, I rest assured," said Roy. "I don't know why Sara gave you the elbow, but I trust you." Roy who wanted to know why Sara gave him the elbow, said, "Truly I myself don't know why she suddenly did this. The last time I saw her, we were in a coffee shop and everything was all right. Believe me that I didn't say anything to her. But she called me last night and said that she didn't want to see me anymore." They were talking that the train arrived and they got on the train. David said, "It's strange for me and I tried a lot to understand why she decided to disrupt her relationship with you, but she didn't say anything to me and just said that she didn't love you and didn't want to see you. During these days Sara's behavior is so strange. There are three days that she didn't go to her work and when I asked her the reason, she said that she handed in her resignation. I don't know why she did this work. She loved her job. She didn't say anything about going on a trip to me, but today I saw an airplane ticket on her desk. The destination of the ticket was Seattle. She has changed a lot during the past days. Anyhow you should not be upset, because this is her wish." "I'm not upset and even if I were, I respect others' opinions and wishes. Everyone has a right to choose. The only thing which I am eager to know is that why she suddenly give me the elbow," said Roy. "Don't be upset. I will ask her later. I really didn't want Sara to disrupt her relationship with you. I tried a lot to change her mind, but I couldn't. It's better to forget about it." Both of them were so happy that nothing could have a negative effect on their intimacy. Although a big grief annoyed him, he made his effort to face this problem logically and in class he tried to pay attention to the lessons. That day Roy dialed Sara's cell phone number several times, but she didn't answer. When he came back home, he dialed Sara's number by internet network and voip system. After two rings, Sara answered. "Hello," said Sara. "Hello, Sara! Please don't cut off the phone," said Roy. "Are you Roy?" "Yes, it's me." "Didn't I tell you that I don't want to have any contacts with you?" "But how is it possible that you change so much during a few days? If you really don't love me,

I won't say anything else and will respect your desire. But I just want to know a thing." "It's very good. You are logical." "It's so difficult for me to forget you, but if you don't love me, I have to forget you." "Do you want to know why I give you the elbow?" "Truly, it makes no difference, but it's interesting for me know how you changed a lot all of a sudden. David told me that you didn't go to your work and you resigned." "Yes, that's right. If anyone else were in my shoes, he or she would do this." "What has happened to you?" "You can not call it a happening, it's better to say luck. It was begun when one of your classmates told me that she wanted to see me. When I went to see her, she told me that she was ready to give me two million dollars and instead, I gave you the elbow and I accepted." "Did you really accept to change me with two million dollars?" "Yes, it's completely reasonable." "What is her name?" "You really like to know her name, don't you?" "Yeah." "But she told me not to tell anyone her name." "Please tell me her name, Sara!" "Okay, maybe in this case you may get off my back. Her name is Kathy Johnson. She gave me two million dollars to disrupt my relationship with you." "Oh, my God. All of these are her fault." "Well, now do you understand why I gave you the elbow? I want to cut off the phone. Leave me alone." "But I love you, Sara! Give it back to her and everything will be okay. Please, Sara!" "I won't do this. Don't call me again." "Sara…Sara…" And Sara cut off the phone. Roy lay on his bed while he didn't even change his clothes. He felt that he didn't have any power to continue his living. He was lying on the bed that his mother knocked on the door and then entered the room and said, "Why didn't you eat your lunch?" "I have no appetite," said Roy. "Is there anything wrong with you?" "No, why do you ask such a question?" "It's obvious from your appearance that you are too upset and anxious." "Oh, no Mom! I will come right now to eat my lunch."

After having lunch, Roy came back to his room and lay on his bed. He came to contradiction in the judgment about his favorite girl very soon. He felt that his pure love to Sara caused her to humiliate him. He blamed himself for this condition. He was deceived by Sara's beauty and appearance. However after several hours of thinking about his feelings and thoughts, he came to this conclusion that the best work was to forget his problems and make himself busy with working. So he first stated continuing working on his project and after that he studied his lessons. Unlike most of the days that time passed so slowly for him, but on that day he felt that time passed more quickly. It was 11o' clock at night and Roy was still working. Roy had forgotten an important issue. But daVinci reminded him to check his email. After his box was opened he saw an email which was sent from Mr. Arthur. He said in that email that according to the request of the current owner of the painting, he was not permitted to tell his name to Roy or anyone else and this was one of the terms of their transaction. He told that despite of this fact that this term was assigned orally between them, he didn't want to break this term. He also added that the reason of assigning this term between them was that the purchaser of the painting was a very sensitive person and he didn't have enough energy to interview with reporters or the fans and he didn't want to face with so many emails and calls which include the suggestion for selling the painting or displaying it at the museum or exhibition. "John! The fat is in the fire. He won't accept to give us the name of painting's owner," said Roy. "What does it mean?" asked daVinci. "It means that we don't have any way to access the painting. It's impossible to have access to that painting according to Mr. Arthur's writing. But our persistence may become effective and he finally accepts to tell us his features." "Yes, it's better to send him another email and say that we want his features." "I'm not sure that he'll agree with our request." "What do you think that we tell him we just want to see the painting from near and don't intend to buy it?" "Don't you think that if we tell Mr. Arthur that we don't want to buy it, he will doubt about us?" "No, even in this case we should propose our request." "So I will send him an email right now and will tell him that we don't want to buy the painting and we just want to see the panting for a short time. Truly speaking, I myself come to this conclusion that we must access to the painting even for a few seconds." "Of course, Roy! I have told you several times that I don't want to get you in trouble, however you are right and we can solve our problem if we have access to the painting for just some seconds." "When you come back to your time, we won't need the painting." After sending that email Roy turned off the computer and fell asleep. He felt that his body and soul were so tired and he must sleep. Unlike the last night that he couldn't sleep till 3:30 in the morning, he fell asleep only a few minutes after he went to his bed. Roy could overcome his moral sufferings by concentrating his mind on his daily works and activities. He could learn important lessons of life during a couple of weeks. Now he knew that he should not judge people according to their appearance. Next day he woke up by the ringing of the clock as everyday. He didn't feel boring at all. After having breakfast and drinking coffee, he went to the university. In his first class with Kathy he didn't say to her that he was aware of what she had done with Sara. In the break he talked to her about that matter and asked her the reason of her unreasonable work. "Kathy! Can you explain a little about that ridiculous work that you had done with Sara?" asked Roy. "I don't understand what you mean," said Kathy. "Stop beating about the bush. Sara had told me everything." "Did she say everything to you?" "Yeah" "I really don't want to interfere in your private life, I just do it for fun. Believe me." "Fun? You really want me to believe that you had done that work just for fun!" "I know that you are angry, but I just told Sara that I was ready to give her two million dollars in order to give you the elbow, but I was kidding with her. Unlike me expectation, Sara considered this as serious and I really gave her the money." "Contrary to your thought, I am not angry of you. I'm happy that you caused me to understand Sara's real nature, but this does not mean that I'm satisfied with you and you must know that you had done a very bad and humiliating work with my life and our friendship won't be the same as the previous." "But, Roy! That was just for fun and it suddenly became serious. Believe me that I'm upset, too." "I don't know what do you think about me or others and it's not important for me that your father is a billionaire. Maybe you think you can buy the people and their lives by money, but I don't think like you and I value them. At least I don't allow myself to disrupt other's lives just for fun and amusement." "Roy! I'm really sorry" "It's not necessary to be sorry, you have done something which caused me to be acquainted with my surrounding people more and I won't trust everyone. You should not expect me to behave you as the previous." Roy said this sentence and went farther from Kathy, and Kathy said several times, "Wait Roy! ...Roy..." But it was useless and Roy made his relationship faint with Kathy. After several hours, Kathy herself became aware that Roy didn't behave her like the past and being sorry was useless. On the way to come back home, Roy remembered that he should check his email. He started checking his email by the laptop. Mr. Arthur sent him a new email. Since David was next to him, he opened that email and signed out quickly. He acted so cautiously. When he got home, before everything he in boxed his emails and read the email which was sent by Mr. Arthur. Mr.

Arthur said in that email that he would not tell him the features of the owner of the painting. Having access to that painting was much more difficult than Roy and daVinci thought. Roy didn't really know how he can access to the painting. After having lunch, he came back to his room. DaVinci was playing. "By the way, Roy! What did you do for the painting?" asked daVinci. "Mr. Arthur won't give us the features of the owner of the painting in any case. I don't know what I can do," said Roy. "It's better to meet Mr. Arthur. Maybe he'll trust us and give us the features of the painting's owner." "I'm not sure it can be useful, but I'll try it. I will make an appointment with him. If we call him today, we may meet him tomorrow or the day after tomorrow. By the way, do you paint this picture?" "Yes, I draw it this morning." "It's very beautiful." Roy hung up that painting on the wall of his room. It was 5o' clock in the afternoon. He went to the kitchen to drink coffee. He made a coup of coffee and went to the living room. "Hi, Dad!" said Roy. "Hi, Roy! How are you?" said Steven. "I'm fine." "By the way, Roy! I want to tell you something." "What?" "Mr. Johnson has invited us to their house." "Really? What a pity!" "Why?" "Because I'm so busy. I don't have any free time to go to this party." "You are kidding! Don't you really have any time to go with us?" "I know that Mr. Johnson is one of your best friends, but I really can not come." "Okay, Roy! It doesn't matter." Then Roy went back to his room. He really didn't want to go to that party. He had bad feelings toward Kathy. Although he didn't really want to go to that party, he felt that his parents may be offended by him. He thought with himself and finally came to this conclusion that he should go there for the sake of hid parents. He concluded that the event between him and Kathy was just related to themselves and not to their parents. He made his decision to go to that party. So he went to his father again and said, "I will go with you to the party tonight, Dad." "Really?" asked Steven. "Yes, I have thought a lot about this and finally come to this conclusion that I should come with you." "I know that you respect us a lot." Then he went to his room and started studying his lessons. Afterwards he changes his clothes and made himself ready for the party. "John! Tonight we are going to go to a party. My mother made your dinner. It's on the kitchen's table. You can eat it whenever you like," said Roy. "Where are you going?" asked daVinci. "One of my father's friends has invited us. If you want, you can come with us." "No thanks, I will stay at home." Then they went to Mr. Johnson's house. Their house was much larger than Roy thought. They entered the house with their car and after parking the car, they went inside the house. There were a number of servants and bodyguards in their house. At last they met Mr. Johnson and his family and after greeting they sat down. For some moments they were silent and they didn't know what to say. It seemed that Roy and Kathy didn't have anything to say. Roy didn't like to talk to Kathy at all. However, he behaved in manner as if he didn't have any problem with Kathy. After one hour, they started eating dinner. After dinner Kathryn sat near Kathy's mother and Steven sat next to Mr. Johnson and Kathy changed her seat and sat exactly beside Roy. Roy didn't know what his reaction should be. Although he didn't hate Kathy, he didn't want to be intimate with a person who annoyed him. Kathy said slowly, "Roy! I know you are upset because of that matter, but everything happened suddenly. I am upset, too. Believe me!" "Although it's useless, I don't expect you to do such a task," said Roy. "That girl had told you a lie. You yourself know it." "Yes, she did, but you didn't have the right to interfere in my private life." "I apologize you and I hope you forget that matter. We can be good friends with each other like our fathers." "Maybe" "By the way, do you want to see my room?" "Yes" "So come with me." Then they went to Kathy's room. Her room was completely different with Roy's room. There was no aquarium or book shelf in her room So many pictures and paintings were hung on her room walls. "Truly speaking, from childhood I love my room more than anywhere else. My world is as small as this room," said Kathy. Then Kathy sat behind her computer desk and turned it on. "Roy, come and sit here," said Kathy. Kathy started showing Roy her childhood and teens photos. She was explaining about the photos and Roy took a look around himself now and then, while he was listening to Kathy. Soon after Roy was sitting behind the computer desk, something attracted him. He saw the painting which he sought for some days on the wall of Kathy's room. "Is this painting genuine, Kathy?" asked Roy. "Yes," said Kathy. "Do you really buy such an expensive painting just for hanging on you room wall?" "You know, Roy! I am interested in this painting a lot. When I look at it, I feel a special comfort. I have intended to buy it from past. Finally I could buy it a couple of weeks ago. Its owner didn't want to sell it, but when I paid him more money, he agreed." "You certainly told its previous owner not to tell others that he sold it to you, didn't you?" "Roy! You are a very strange person, how did you know that?" "Forget about it." Roy was so happy as if a new power full of hope and happiness was created in him. Having access to the painting meant finishing the major problem of his life. "I am interested in paintings, especially daVinci's works. For this reason that day I invited you to the exhibition that you also enjoy the beauty of that painting. From the time I have bought the painting, I feel a special happiness," said Kathy. "Can I ask you something?" asked Roy. "Yes, of course," said Kathy. "I know that my request is a little selfishly and unreasonable, but..." "Say it, Roy!" "Can you lend me the painting for one day?" "Okay, but would you please say why do you want it?" "Oh, don't worry. I won't damage it. I need it just for one day or maybe some hours." "But you didn't answer my question." "I just want to see it more." "Okay, whenever you like, you can borrow it from me." "Can you lend it to me tomorrow?" "Yes." "Be sure that I won't damage it. But please don't say anything to your parents about this." "Rest assured that they won't understand anything about this matter." Afterwards they watched the photos again and then went out of Kathy's room. Roy still couldn't believe that he met the owner of the painting so simply. But he didn't want to risk anymore and made his decision to borrow the painting at that night. And Kathy accepted to lend him the painting and put it in a silver cover and gave it to Roy. Roy felt that Kathy has done a very great work for him and he didn't nurse a grudge against her. His prejudgments about Kathy were wrong and Kathy was still considered as a good friend for Roy. That night when Roy came back home, he put the painting in a safe place and then told the story for daVinci. Both of them were so happy that they could at last have access to the painting. Although Roy liked daVinci, he felt that he should return him to his time as soon as possible. "John, I want to tell you something. I want to return you to your time up to some later minutes," said Roy. "But why so quickly? Don't you think it's better to wait some more days?" said daVinci. "I know that, but we should do it in any case. You are a genius who belongs to every people of the world and I should not think about myself. The only way of compensating for these problems is to return you to your time." "I understand you, Roy! But it was not your fault." "We should do it right now. I don't want to miss this opportunity. Everything may happen in future. Something bad may happen for the painting, or necklace or even you yourself." "I myself want to come back." Roy brought out daVinci's clothes from under the bed and gave them to him to wear his own clothes. He finally became ready and Roy brought the painting and necklace in order to start the task. Then he and daVinci stood in front of the painting, but he didn't still put on the necklace. "I hope you apologize me that during this period I called you with this pen name," said Roy. "Oh, no I should apologize you since during this period I made you worried," said daVinci. "I like you to stay with me more." "I had good feelings during these past days. You are a very good friend for me." "You, too. Are you ready?" "Yes, but can I ask you a question?" "Yes, of course." "What do you want to do with the necklace after you'll return me?" "I want to go to a jeweler and ask him to make an imitation stone like this, and then hide the stone in a safe place." "So you think about it." "Yes, are you ready for going?" "Yes." Then Roy put on the necklace and while daVinci was standing next to him, he looked at the painting. After some seconds they transferred to daVinci's time. Afterwards daVinci went farther from Roy and Roy put the green side of the necklace at the back and the blue one in front and then he returned to his own time that is 21 century and year 2006. He quickly removed the necklace from his neck and put it in his drawer and also put the painting in its cover. Now he was relaxed after a period of unexpected problems and worries. He was lying on his bed and the last events were reviewing in his mind. He could not believe that the problems which made him frightened were now solved. Although the next day was holiday, he woke up early in the morning. He didn't feel tired at all and after brushing his teeth and having breakfast, he started seriously doing his works with self confidence. Roy's parents who understood daVinci or Mr. Walker's absence asked him where he went. And he told them that the period which his doctor was assigned was finished and he must return to his family.

Then Roy called Kathy to give back the painting. Kathy didn't need the painting on that day, but Roy told him that he wanted to give back the painting just on that day. They made an appointment and then Kathy came and took the picture from Roy. In the middle of the day, Roy could finish his project. He sent it to the email of that company and they paid him the money according to the contract. They suggested Roy to have more cooperation with them, but he didn't accept it. Money was not so important for him. The thing which was important for him was that he was able to use his skills in solving his problems and in critical conditions. Roy' life has become calm again, but now he had more self confidence and bravery to continue his life. He needed his parents' affection more than before. He spent several hours with them watching TV. While they were watching TV, they faced strange news. Of course it wasn't strange for Roy. The robbers, who had stolen a number of the paintings, now gave them back. They gave them back safe and sound, while the exhibition was closed. Although it was strange for everyone, they were happy that the paintings were returned to their place. Then Roy came back to his room and studied his lessons. It was 12:30 that Kathryn called Roy for lunch. After having lunch, he played his favorite games. Afterwards he fell asleep. It was 6:30 when he woke up. He made himself ready for going to the university. He took the necklace and put it in his pocket in order to show it to a jeweler. He didn't want to face unexpected events again. He removed its chain and put it in the drawer again and just took its stone. That day he had good feelings at the university. In the third break Kathy invited Roy for drink. They were sitting opposite to each other and drinking coffee. None of them knew what to say. In Roy's opinion Kathy was considered just as a good friend for him, but their relationship was different for Kathy. After

Roy's loving relationship with Sara was disrupted, he was pessimistic toward girls and he didn't think about marriage. But the intimate relations between Roy and Kathy were not considered just as a friendship and Kathy's behavior had indicated that she chose Roy as her future husband. Although Roy understood this fact, he never tried to think about it. But when Kathy told him that she loved him, Roy couldn't escape the reality or deny it. "Roy, I want to tell you an important matter. How can I tell you? I…I love you and I want you to be my husband," said Kathy. "Oh, Kathy, I know you, but I should think about it." Roy was a little perplexed. He had a bad experience in love recently and he didn't want to think about another love. However he didn't have any bad feelings toward Kathy. He couldn't even imagine that Kathy wanted to marry him. It was too unexpected for him. In class all the time he thought about Kathy and her behaviors. On the way to come back home, he went to a jewelry store and showed the stone to the jeweler. That man first surveyed the stone and told Roy that he could make an imitation up to two weeks later and according to his order make a gold chain and deliver it to Roy. After recording its size and features, he gave back the stone to Roy. Roy had decided to hide the genuine stone of the necklace forever. He was so happy that his problems were finished. But now his mind was busy at Kathy's suggestion. He thought about this matter foe a couple of days and he came to this conclusion that Kathy could be a good wife for him. He would graduate next year and he should marry sooner or later. Soon he understood that he fell in love with Kathy again. A couple of days passed. Kathy invited Roy to a coffee shop for talking about the current matter. It was 8:30 at night and Roy wore his clothes and he was ready to go to the coffee shop. Roy had succeeded in the driving license test and now he had a driving license and his father also had bought him a car. Unlike everyday that he used to go by taxi or metro, this time he went by his personal car. He arrived there on time. Kathy was waiting for him. After greeting, they sat behind a table and then ordered the drink. Kathy started talking. Some days had passed from the day Kathy proposed her suggestion to Roy and this made her worried. She thought that his answer would be negative. So she tried to say everything to Roy to change his mind. "Roy, I know what you think about me. You think I'm a rich and spoilt girl that money is just important for me and I don't pay attention to other's feelings. But it's not true. From my childhood I have grown in a cage. I never can go out without bodyguards and anti bullet car. I always feel that I am in a cage. I always want to be as the usual people. I wish my father wouldn't be a billionaire," said Kathy. "No, Kathy! I don't think so about you. At first I thought you are proud of your money, but when I was acquainted with you more, I understood that it wasn't true and you are such a trustworthy girl," said Roy. "Most of the time I wish I were not existed. I don't know why I'm telling you these things..." "It doesn't matter. Even if we won't marry, we can be good friends with each other. And you can trust me." "Thanks Roy! Did you think about my suggestion?" "Yes." "So what is your answer?" "Well, I've thought a lot about it and then came to this conclusion that I love you and need you, too." "Very well Roy! I'm so happy of that." "But we should tell our parents this issue and be engaged for some time." "Okay" "What do you think about starting a new life from now?" "What do you mean?" "I mean tell your bodyguards to go home and I will get you home, of course after we wander around the city." "To tell you the truth it needs so much bravery since I've never go out without bodyguard. But I will accept it for the sake of you." Both of them were happy. "By the way, Roy! You didn't have a driving license, so how can you drive?" asked Kathy. "I didn't have up to some days ago, but now I have. This car is my father's gift for accepting in the driving license test," said Roy. A couple of days later Roy and Kathy became engaged formally and after one year both of them graduated from the university and they married each other.

www.ingramcontent.com/pod-product-compliance
Lightning Source LLC
Chambersburg PA
CBHW071159260626
47162CB00003B/1107